Last Dance on Holladay Street

Last Dance on Holladay Street

Elisa Carbone

Alfred A. Knopf
New York

THIS IS A BORZOI BOOK PUBLISHED BY ALFRED A. KNOPF

Copyright © 2005 by Elisa Carbone
Jacket illustration copyright © 2005 by Hadley Hooper
All rights reserved under International and Pan-American Copyright Conventions. Published in the United States of America by Alfred A. Knopf, an imprint of Random House Children's Books, a division of Random House, Inc., New York, and simultaneously in Canada by Random House of Canada Limited, Toronto. Distributed by Random House, Inc., New York.

KNOPF, BORZOI BOOKS, and the colophon are registered trademarks of Random House, Inc.

www.randomhouse.com/teens

Library of Congress Cataloging-in-Publication Data
Carbone, Elisa Lynn.
Last dance on Holladay Street / Elisa Carbone. —1st ed.
p.   cm.
SUMMARY: In 1878, thirteen-year-old Eva seeks her birth mother in Colorado, only to find the city and her mother are not what she imagines.
ISBN 0-375-82896-6 (trade) — ISBN 0-375-92896-0 (lib. bdg.)
1. Colorado—History—1876–1950—Juvenile fiction. 2. African Americans—Juvenile fiction. [1. Colorado—History—1876–1950—Fiction. 2. African Americans—Fiction. 3. Frontier and pioneer life—Colorado—Fiction.] I. Title.
PZ7.C1865Las 2005
[Fic]—dc22
2004010314

Printed in the United States of America
March 2005
10 9 8 7 6 5 4 3 2 1
First Edition

FOR JACKIE

Eva's hands shook as she opened the small wooden box. What would Mama Kate think if she knew how often she peeked in here these days? That she had already given her up for dead? But Eva couldn't help herself. Carefully she unfolded the worn, yellowing envelope and read the return address—again. *Sadie Lewis, 518 Holladay Street, Denver, Colorado.* And the letter—read it for the hundredth time. *Desember 1865. This is for the child. Plez do not rite back.* The letter was now thirteen years old, sent that first Christmas. Each year since then the envelopes had come, and the money, but no more letters.

If it were not for that devilish mare of Mr. Harper's, Eva wouldn't even be in this predicament. If a horse could be hung for murder, she would have strung up that mare. It happened just a year ago. Eva was on her way from the house to the barn with slop for the hog when she heard the mare's shrill whinny, then Daddy Walter's curses, and knew the mare had hurt him. She dropped the slop bucket and went running.

Daddy Walter held a rag to his bleeding hand.

"Daddy!" she cried, and tried to see how bad it was.

"It's nothing, sweetheart," Daddy Walter said. "She didn't

1

like me driving nails into her hooves, so she decided to drive a nail back into my hand, make me see how it feels."

But the blood soaking into that white rag made Eva's stomach queasy. "We should get you bandaged proper," she said.

"Mr. Harper needs his mare back by this afternoon. I'll finish up here, then I'll come to the house and you and Mama Kate can fix me up with all the salves and tinctures you can find." He grinned through the pain.

Six days later he took to his bed with a fever and headache and his jaw so stiff he could barely speak. The doctor said it was tetanus and there was nothing to be done. Eva and Mama Kate cared for him. They spooned thin soup through his clenched jaws and tried to hold him down when he thrashed and choked and cursed as if the devil himself had entered his bones. The day he finally lay still, it was a relief. Even white folks they hardly knew came to his funeral and said nice things about him, as if having a black man in town had been an honor. After that, the house was much too quiet, much too empty. Eva kept thinking she heard Daddy Walter's voice or footsteps or laugh. Then she would remember.

If it wasn't for that mare, Mama Kate would be leaving her with Daddy Walter. Instead she was leaving her to a woman who couldn't even stomach a thank-you letter from the child she gave away.

Eva carefully folded the old letter, put it back in its envelope, and closed the box. Then she went into the yard, where Mama Kate was hanging the clothes they'd just washed—not their own clothes, but their neighbors', washed and ironed to bring in cash.

"Mama Kate, let me finish up here," Eva said, taking a pair of heavy men's dungarees from her. "Please go sit in the shade and rest."

"I can't rest all day," Mama Kate objected.

But Eva took her hand, led her over to the three-legged wash stool, and sat her down. "Just talk to me while I hang these. I'll be done in no time."

At least while school was out for the summer, Eva wanted to do as much of the work on the homestead as she could. The more Mama Kate rested, Eva reasoned, the better her health would be. Later Eva would take their horse and buckboard and ride the two miles into town to deliver the clean clothes. Then she would stop at Mr. Harper's store, not to buy anything, but to pay down their debt from last winter. She would ride back home as the late sun turned the prairie grasses to gold. She'd give the cow her evening milking, shut the chickens up for the night, and help Mama Kate make supper.

They heard a woman's cheery voice call from the front gate. "*Buon giorno!* Good morning!"

Eva squinted into the bright sunshine and smiled as their neighbor, Mrs. Santini, came into the yard. Mrs. Santini didn't keep a polite distance the way the other white folks in town did. She always kissed them hello and good-bye—on both cheeks. And Eva liked the way she often had dirt under her fingernails from working in her garden and smelled of the sweet basil she grew in a flowerpot on her windowsill.

"I say to myself, who knows? Maybe they starving in there," said Mrs. Santini. Her arms were filled with packages. "I bring you piece chicken—my husband say is too much for him—and onions and tomatoes from my garden. Come, Eva, I teach you to make a nice cacciatore."

Eva knew Mrs. Santini was joking about them starving, but the truth was, she and Mama Kate hadn't had meat in a long time. Eva had gone to bed hungry more than once this week, though things weren't nearly as bad as last winter.

The three of them went into the kitchen, and Eva took her place beside Mrs. Santini at the table. Together they chopped the vegetables and hacked up the raw chicken with a cleaver. Mama Kate put on the kettle for tea.

"The secret is, you cook slow," said Mrs. Santini, leaning toward Eva conspiratorially. "The tomatoes and onions, they make a sauce, and everybody think you a big chef from Italy."

"Between what you've taught her and what I've taught her, this girl is a fine cook," Mama Kate said proudly.

Eva gathered up what they'd chopped, put it all in a pot, then ladled water over it from the water crock.

"Put some salt, Eva—not too much," Mrs. Santini said. "Ah!" Her face lit up. She pulled a handful of deep green leaves out of her apron pocket. "*Basilico*. You add later." She gave the basil leaves to Eva, and their rich aroma filled the air.

Eva opened the stove and used the bellows to bring the fire up just a little. Then she put a lid on the pot and left the chicken to stew.

Mrs. Santini took Eva's face in her hands, beaming at her. "*È tanta in gamba, questa bellissima ragazza!*" she exclaimed.

"What did I do this time?" Eva asked. She was always suspicious when Mrs. Santini had outbursts in Italian.

"I say what a capable girl you are, and so beautiful, too!" she said.

Eva blushed.

"She is, isn't she?" Mama Kate said, her eyes soft with love.

Please don't say it, Mama Kate, Eva begged silently. *Don't say you wish you could be here to watch me grow up. I don't want to cry in front of Mrs. Santini.*

But Mama Kate just smiled, and Eva poured the tea. The two women settled into conversation about their gardens, the drought, the high price of flour, and Eva sat to sip tea and listen. She noticed that Mrs. Santini had the sleeves of her dress pushed up to her elbows, and so she quietly devised a way to answer a question she'd had for some time. She pushed up the sleeve of her own dress, then stealthily, so as not to attract attention, slid her arm over next to Mrs. Santini's. There it was, just as she had suspected. Mrs. Santini's arm was actually *darker* than her own. Daddy Walter had been dark as molasses and Mama Kate was brown-skinned. If Eva hadn't been told from early on that she was adopted, she certainly would have wondered where she got her coloring from—long wavy hair and all.

Who was this light-skinned "blood" mother, Sadie Lewis? And what did Eva's older sister look like—the sister who, for some unexplained reason, this mother had been able to keep? Mama Kate said all she knew of the sister was that her name was Pearl and she was still in diapers when Eva was born. Eva also sometimes wondered about the father no one ever made mention of. But trying to think of anyone else as "Daddy" or "Mama" only sent knives into Eva's heart. She scooted over next to Mama Kate and laid her head on her shoulder. Mama Kate stroked her hair gently.

She's here now, Eva thought. *I won't move from this spot and she'll always be with me.*

Mama Kate suddenly erupted with a fit of coughing. Eva ran to the crock and brought her a glass of water. The coughing eased, but not before Eva saw the bright red blood caught in Mama Kate's handkerchief.

Eva searched Mrs. Santini's eyes for an answer—a better answer than "You'll have to be brave and strong." She wanted an answer like "Here is medicine to cure her" or even "My husband say you can stay here with us."

Instead Mrs. Santini broke the news that her husband had decided to try his luck at the new mines opening near Georgetown, way up in the mountains past Denver.

Three days later Mrs. Santini stopped in to say good-bye. Tearfully she kissed them one last time, then left riding atop the wagon next to her husband, with the sweet basil plant sitting between them on the wooden seat. And the consumption, true to its name, continued to eat Mama Kate up from the inside.

Eva hiked out into the prairie with a basket and pried up the flat, dried cow pies to use for fuel. The September nights had become chilly, but Mama Kate said they'd better not buy coal from Mr. Harper until they'd paid more on their debt.

Eva stepped over the thorny cacti, holding her dress down against a strong wind bent on billowing it up. Suddenly she felt prickling on her bare skin, as if the wind was filled with tiny needles. She peered into the distance and saw smoke, gray-brown and moving fast. Was there a fire? The wind needles hit harder—they *hurt*. Were they hot cinders? Then, in an instant, she knew what it was. Dust storm.

She ran. Her way home could disappear in minutes. And the animals had to be shut in the barn, and Mama Kate—Lord, how would she breathe in all that dust?

Eva reached the yard but could barely find the gate. Swirling gray-brown dust, thick as fog, stung her eyes and caught in her throat. She held her apron against her mouth and nose. Where was Mama Kate!?

"Get in there!" Mama Kate's voice rose over the howl of wind.

Eva found her, wielding a rake, driving their slow-witted milk cow into the barn.

"Mama Kate, *you* get inside!" Eva shouted. She shoved the cow's rump until she was in the barn, then secured the barn doors and followed her mother into the house.

Mama Kate's coughing racked her whole body. Eva quickly dipped a rag in clean water and gave it to her to breathe through. Then she slammed the shutters and set to work hanging damp sheets over the windows and stuffing every crack with rags until the house was dark as night and Mama Kate had to light the kerosene lamp. Outside, it sounded as if the world was being swept away.

"I got the horse and the chickens in before it got real bad," Mama Kate said, but Eva's eyes were fixed on the rag Mama Kate held to her mouth. It had begun to drip blood. Eva's head swam and she braced herself against the windowsill. "You stayed outside too long!" she cried. She took the rag away, gave Mama Kate a clean one, then slumped into a kitchen chair.

Mama Kate came to Eva and stroked her cheek. "Baby, you know the good Lord has got plans for me and there's nobody who can interfere with that."

"I don't *want* His plans!" Eva pounded her fist on the table.

Mama Kate shook her head. "Don't be disagreeing with the Lord." She sat close to Eva, held her shoulders, and rocked her. "Remember that winter when the snow blew so deep we couldn't get out for days? It's about as dark in here right now as it was then. Remember how Daddy Walter read to us from the

Rocky Mountain News, only he changed the stories to make them silly?"

Eva smiled, remembering.

"He surely made Saint Peter laugh on his way into heaven, that man," said Mama Kate.

"And you taught me to make biscuits with burnt flour gravy since all we had in the house was lard and flour and salt," Eva said. "And then we ran out of salt, so we used gunpowder instead."

Mama Kate nodded. "That first time you burnt the flour a little *too* much, but then you got the hang of it," she said. She pulled away from Eva and looked into her face. "Go get me my sewing, baby. We all got our journeys to go on, and it's time I got you ready for yours."

Mama Kate went to the bed, reached under the mattress, and pulled out something that glinted in the light of the kerosene lamp—a silver dollar. "Come scoot your knees up here," she said. She pulled the hem of Eva's petticoat onto her lap, ripped out a little of the stitching, then began to secure the silver dollar into the hem with neat, tiny stitches. "Don't use this unless there's *nothing* else you can do," she told her.

"Mama, are you sending me away *now*?" Eva asked. She felt tears press behind her eyes.

"Not until the Lord decides it's time, baby. Mr. Harper knows to buy you a train ticket, and he'll take what's left on the homestead—the tools and the animals—to pay for our debt at his store and your train fare." She bent over her sewing. "And I'll still be watching over you, so you make me glad, you hear?"

Eva nodded.

"You're the first one in this family born free," Mama Kate told her. "Wherever you go, you be proud and strong so it's clear that you know in your bones that you're free—that nobody better try to push you somewhere you don't want to go. You understand?"

"Yes, Mama," Eva answered. Mama Kate's words made it sound as if she was about to embark on some grand adventure, leaving on the train with Mama Kate's blessing. If only Mama Kate would be there to welcome her home when she came back to tell her stories.

"Now, this Sadie Lewis, I reckon she must be a good woman, seeing how she wanted a good life for you."

Sadie Lewis. Hearing the name aloud tied Eva's stomach into a tight knot.

"I remember the day—it was thirteen years ago now—me and your daddy decided to ride into Denver to see the sights, and that woman, a friend of Miss Sadie's, saw us and said she had a beautiful colored baby whose mama couldn't take care of her. Well, me and Daddy Walter, we'd waited so long for a child, we figured we were too old and gave up. But just like with Abraham and his wife, Sarah, the good Lord decided we weren't too old after all. We were so thrilled to have you!" She held Eva's chin in her hand. "I still am. Thankful for you every day."

Eva wrinkled up her nose. "Were you thankful for me the day I used cow pies to make 'stew' in your good cooking pot?"

Mama Kate laughed, and her laughing turned to coughing, yet her eyes danced with humor. "And Daddy Walter had to pretend to be angry with you?"

"That was no pretend whipping I got!" Eva said indignantly.

"It was for your own good—for *our* own good. We didn't want to always be wondering what we'd find in the stew! That's when I figured I'd better teach you to cook right quick." She finished her stitching and bit the thread. "Help me to bed, sugar," she said.

Eva propped Mama Kate up against the pillows and sat next to the bed. Outside, the dust storm was loud as ever, and thin dust swirled in the light of the lamp, but Eva felt cozy and safe sitting here, her fingers entwined with Mama Kate's strong brown hands.

"If I had kin back in South Carolina to send you to, I would. But my sister—your aunt Linnie—is the only one left, and she'd never be able to feed you. Every letter I get from her is hungrier than the last, with her still working for the old master all these years after the war. She says she's in debt to him now, and her crops go to feed him instead of her.

"And I've got no one to send you to from Daddy Walter's

kin in Kentucky—they all got sold off before the war, and he never found a one of them. Not that he tried hard. I don't think he wanted any chains holding him back from coming out here. Family can be like that, you know—chains holding you to responsibilities and such.

"But I think this here Sadie Lewis has got on her feet by now. She sent enough money last Christmas to buy the gingham and lace for your new Sunday dress. And I hope you'll tell her that Daddy Walter and Mama Kate took good care of her baby for a time."

Eva clutched Mama Kate's hand tighter. "But you don't have to send me to her *yet*, right, Mama?"

"Only when it's time," Mama Kate said. She closed her eyes and laid her head back against the pillows.

Eva changed into her nightgown and combed out her braid. Then she extinguished the lamp and climbed into bed beside Mama Kate. She felt her mother's loving touch on her hair. There was no need to worry herself sick over this Sadie Lewis, she decided—not yet. She relaxed and allowed her eyes to blur with sleep.

When Eva awoke, it was quiet outside. The dust storm had subsided, and early morning sunlight peeked in through the cracks where the rags had fallen out. Eva felt Mama Kate's hand still resting on her head. She didn't want to wake her, so she reached up to gently lift her mother's arm. But the moment

Eva touched her mother's skin, a chill went through her. It was waxy and cold. She jerked back to see Mama Kate's jaw hanging open, her eyes staring wide and blank.

"No, Mama Kate!" Eva cried. "I wasn't *ready!*" She reached out, wanting to shake Mama Kate, to wake her, to bring life back into her. But she stopped; she couldn't stand to feel that cold hardness again. "I wanted you to stay!" Eva wailed. She bit her hand to hold back sobs, then gave in, closed her eyes, let the tears stream down her face.

I'll be watching over you, so you make me glad, you hear? Eva remembered the words, tried to hear Mama Kate's voice telling her, promising. She lifted the bedsheet and pulled it up to cover Mama Kate's still face.

"Can you watch over me from heaven?" Eva whispered. She shivered. Her own body had turned cold from weeping. She washed her face in the washbowl, put on her dress, and braided her hair into one long, thick braid. Then she found Daddy Walter's old carpetbag and loaded her few belongings into it. When she was done, she stood looking at what had been her home: the squat, friendly stove with cook pans and ladles hanging above it, the wash bucket in the corner, awaiting the next wash day. "I'm never coming back," she said aloud to the quiet room. Then she put on her hat and shawl and started on her way to Mr. Harper's store to tell him what had happened and to ask for that train ticket.

The train now barreled over the sunlit plains, past hills blotched with pale green soap weed. Eva sat in one of the hard wooden seats, staring out the window. She felt as if she had drifted through the past several days. She'd stayed at the Harpers', where everyone had tiptoed around her as if she were a tinderbox and might explode into tears at any moment. But she only cried quietly at night, when she knew the two Harper girls were already asleep. The funeral had been small, with just a few folks joining Eva and the reverend. Eva figured everyone in town knew she was leaving soon, so why bother to make themselves sad by coming to see a girl bury her mother? They put Mama Kate to rest in the graveyard north of town, next to Daddy Walter, far from where the Big Sandy Creek could flood in spring. And now Eva was leaving it all behind.

Denver had always been just over the next rise in the prairie, yet Eva had never been there. She had sometimes wondered about that glittering town, where ladies wore silk dresses and men carried pearl-tipped canes. Mama Kate and Daddy Walter had told her about it—of streets filled with people and noise like a roaring in your ears. They'd said they would take her someday, but it had always been more important to buy new shoes or wool for new shawls than to spend their money on train tickets just to go *see* a place.

The train stopped in the small, dusty prairie towns: River Bend, Agate, Deer Trail. On the depot platform in Deer Trail, Eva saw a large pile of buffalo bones, gleaming white in the sun. She rested her forehead against the window and watched as two men loaded the bones into a freight car on the other side of the tracks. At school her teacher had talked about the bones, how this was all that was left of the thousands of buffalo that once roamed the plains. They'd been slaughtered, her teacher said, to make room for grazing cattle. Now their bones were being gathered and shipped back east to be made into buttons and ground into fertilizer. Her teacher said it was like new life coming from death, but Eva thought it was just plain death. She turned away from the window, and the train started up again.

Before she saw Denver, Eva saw the mountains. They rose like great gray monsters that, if angered, might loosen themselves from their perch and come rolling down, crushing everything in their path. Lord, Eva thought, would she be living in their shadow from now on?

The Platte River came into view. The September dryness had turned it into a small stream in the middle of its wide riverbed, with parched-looking cottonwoods crowded along its banks. The train rushed past the first houses on the edge of town: low-slung, unpainted, drab brown houses.

"Next stop, Denver!" the conductor shouted.

Denver, you're not so grand after all, Eva thought.

She picked up her bag and adjusted her hat. She'd worn her Sunday dress and planned to tell Sadie Lewis, "My mama used the Christmas money you sent to make me this dress. I know you never wanted thank-you letters from me, but I reckon you can't refuse a thank-you in person."

The train slowed as it entered the train yard and chugged to a halt in front of the huge brick station. Already, out her window, Eva saw more people than she'd ever seen in one place.

She stepped into the aisle. Immediately people began jostling, pushing toward the doors and shoving her in the process. What confusion! She elbowed her way into the crowd, following the flow to the end of the car and down the steep train steps.

On the platform she entered the real mayhem. Here people rushed in different directions, either toward the trains, which sat spewing smoke in the rail yard, or into the yawning doorway of the train station. Eva made her way into the station. Inside, noise echoed off the cavernous walls and ceiling as hawkers shouted out their wares and workmen pushed rickety wheeled carts.

Eva blinked as her eyes adjusted to the dim lighting. She didn't even see the cart until it was upon her. A heavy wheel rolled over her foot.

"Owwwch!" she cried.

The man pushing the cart was a Chinese in a white tunic

and loose pants. He shouted something at her that she guessed meant "Watch where you're going next time" and pushed his cart toward a double doorway that Eva thought must lead to the city streets. Mr. Harper had given her a little pocket money and said to spend it on a hack if she needed to. Maybe she could find one out there. She wanted nothing more than to be driven away from all of this noise and confusion.

Eva switched the carpetbag to her other hand, gritted her teeth against the pain, and limped toward the double doors.

"Tillie!" she heard someone call nearby.

Wouldn't it be wonderful, she thought, if *she* were Tillie? She wished she had someone to meet her and take her to Holladay Street.

"Tillie!" The voice was even closer now.

Eva continued to make her way toward the doorway until a hand closed on her shoulder.

"Tillie, didn't you hear me calling you?"

Eva whirled around and found herself face to face with a handsome young white man. He was wearing a fine suit and smiling in a very friendly way.

"It's wonderful to see you!" he said. He was looking at her as if she were some long-awaited family friend.

Eva's eyes widened. "I'm sorry, sir," she said, "but you must have me confused with someone else."

The man cocked his head quizzically. "Well, I'll have to have a word with the photographer, then. You're the spitting image of the photographs I've seen of Tillie." He bowed politely, taking off his hat. "I'm Zeke. Zeke Stauder."

This young man thought she was someone wealthy enough to have a photograph made of herself? She tried not to look too surprised. "I'm Eva," she said, flattered by his attention. "Eva Wilkins."

"An honor to make your acquaintance," said Zeke. "May I help you to find a hack?"

"Yes, please!" she said with relief.

"Here, let me carry that for you." Zeke took her bag and offered his arm. Shyly Eva linked her arm through his. She hoped her Sunday dress and her best manners made her seem more sophisticated than just a farm girl. Her foot was feeling better, and she managed to walk without limping.

The crowd had begun to thin out. From outside in the rail yard Eva heard a conductor shout, "All aboard!" An old black man, tall and lanky, bent over his broom and swept the wooden floor near where Eva and Zeke walked.

"Or perhaps you're hungry after your long trip," Zeke said. "Would you like to stop at a fruit stand first?"

Eva was hungry *and* thirsty. The thought of an apple or a pear made her mouth water. She was about to say, "Yes, thank you" when the old man with the broom came so close he nearly swept the shine off Zeke's boots.

"*Excuse* me," Zeke said pointedly, and glared at the man.

The man gave Zeke a steady stare, then went back to sweeping.

"Denver has some of the world's finest fruit stands and ice cream shops, you know," Zeke continued.

"Ice cream *shops*?" Eva asked in amazement. She had tasted ice cream just once, at the country fair. But to think, here they had *shops* that sold ice cream!

The old man seemed to buzz around them like an annoying bee, always needing to sweep right where they were walking. Then suddenly he was in front of them, drawn up to his full height, the broom held sideways to block their path.

Eva waited for Zeke to demand that he step aside. But before Zeke could speak, the old man, his dark eyes set in a determined gaze, said, "She ain't but twelve or thirteen years old, and the marshal is right over yonder"—he nodded at a knot of men gathered nearby—"and I'm ready to have a word with him."

Zeke seemed to shrink inside his expensive suit. He peered across the station as if he'd just recognized someone he knew, dropped Eva's bag on the floor, and hurried off without saying a word.

"Why did you have to chase him off?" Eva blurted out. "He was *helping* me!"

The old man looked at her calmly. "If he was so nice, then what happened to Tillie?"

Eva frowned. What *had* happened to Tillie?

The man shook his head. "You listen to me. If you're going to take two steps in Denver without losing all your money and maybe your self-respect, too, you'd better go sit on that bench over there and wait until I'm done with these floors, and then I'll take you to your kin. . . ." He hesitated. "You do have kin you're coming to visit, don't you?"

Eva wasn't sure of the right answer. The unknown Sadie Lewis certainly didn't *feel* like her kin. Her hesitation seemed to anger the old man.

"Does your mama know you're here?" he asked sharply.

Again Eva didn't know how to answer. Mama Kate had promised to watch over her, but was she watching every moment? Did she know Eva had arrived safely in Denver? And now Sadie Lewis was supposed to be her new mama, but of course she had no idea Eva had arrived.

This time her hesitation seemed to light a fire under the man. He pointed one long dark finger at her, trembling. "Now, if you're a runaway I'm ready to put you right back on that train and send you on home—"

"I'm *not* a runaway!" Eva interrupted him. At least she could say *this* with assurance. "I have an address I need to get to. If you would help me, sir, I would be very grateful."

The man calmed and nodded. "My apologies, miss," he said. "I didn't even introduce myself. Stonewall Smith. People call me Mr. Stonewall."

"Eva Wilkins," Eva said, and gave a slight curtsy.

Mr. Stonewall smiled. "I see you've been properly brought up. Stay away from the Denver riffraff and you'll be just fine."

And so Eva sat on a bench and waited while he finished his sweeping. On the wall behind her hung a human skull with a cigar in its mouth and a hunting cap on its head. If she had been looking for signs, for superstitious messages, she might have taken the skull to be a bad omen. And she would have been right.

"What's that?" Eva pointed upward at the skull.

"A deterrent," said Mr. Stonewall.

Eva had read the sign above the skull—THIS IS THE LAST MAN WHO SPAT ON THE FLOOR—but she couldn't make sense of it.

"Folks used to make a pastime of spitting on this floor—the one I've got to clean," said Mr. Stonewall. "Mr. Franklin Pierce, the station agent—he's named after President Franklin Pierce—he put up signs, PLEASE USE SPITTOONS, but that didn't do no good. So one day he goes to the Mount Prospect Cemetery—to the part where they bury folks who've got no one to care that they're dead—and digs up this here skull. That did the trick."

Eva gave the skull a sideways look. She wondered if it had been a man or a woman. "Why the hat and the cigar?" she asked.

Mr. Stonewall stood his broom up in a corner next to a mop and bucket. "Soon as Mr. Pierce hangs up the skull, see, the night agent says he hears haunting noises all through the station at night: chattering and whistling and such," he explained. "Some folks even say they seen a specter, skinny as a snake, missing the fingers on one hand, lurking around the station."

A shiver ran across Eva's shoulders as if the specter had touched her.

"Mr. Pierce, he doesn't believe in no ghosts, so he says maybe the skull is cold, that's why it's chattering, so he puts the warm hunting cap on its head and then sticks the cigar in its mouth and wires the mouth shut so it can't whistle no more."

"Did that stop the haunting noises?" Eva asked.

Mr. Stonewall shook his head. "Nope. The night agent quit, and the next night agent says he hears chattering and whistling, so he quits. The man who works at night now is mostly deaf, so I suspect he'll be here awhile, at least until he sees that skinny ghost with no fingers floating around."

Just then two men carrying a coffin walked by, looking lost.

"You need to send that back east?" Mr. Stonewall called to them. They both nodded, and Mr. Stonewall directed them to the eastbound train. To Eva he said, "Folks flock out here like sheep—those fool eastern doctors tell them the dry air gets rid of consumption. I think some of those eastbound trains got more dead folks on them than live ones."

"I could have told them there's nothing magic in the air out here for curing consumption," Eva said darkly.

"And they wouldn't listen," said Mr. Stonewall. He picked up her bag and led her out of the dingy station into the bright sunshine.

The sign on the corner said Wazee and 21st streets. Everywhere there were people, horses, carts, wagons. A few buildings lined up along the street: houses, a church, a grocery, a saloon.

The wooden plank sidewalks clattered with footsteps. There were cowhands in spurs and fringed rawhide pants, miners in their candle-wax-splattered hats and heavy boots, and business-men in fine suits and top hats. There were black men and white men, Mexicans and Chinese. She saw two Indian men riding potbellied horses slowly down the dirt street, their long hair braided with feathers and bits of fur. They carried rifles cradled in their laps. Eva stared, wide-eyed.

"No need to worry about them," Mr. Stonewall said, fol-lowing her gaze to the two Indians. "They're Utes—right peace-ful most of the time. Used to be an Indian agency in Denver where they got provisions. It closed a couple years ago, but they still come to trade."

Eva shook her head. "It's not just them," she said. "It's . . . everything."

Mr. Stonewall laughed. "You're quite a hayseed, ain't you?"

Eva looked around, taking it all in. "And they're nearly all men," she said. "Where are the *women*?"

"This is a man's town," said Mr. Stonewall. "It's the mines and the cattle running that make it a town at all. The miners and cowhands come in for supplies and entertainment and such. There's a few good women at home, and the rest are on Holla-day Street."

"Holladay Street," Eva said brightly. "That's where I need to go."

Mr. Stonewall scowled at her. "Now you need to forget anything that scoundrel Zeke told you. He's nothing but a recruiter, and whatever job he said you could get on Holladay Street is not one you want. You ain't going *near* Holladay Street, Miss Eva."

Before Eva could object, he disappeared into a saloon and told her to wait outside. He emerged a minute later with a glass of water. "Bartender's a friend of mine," he said. "I know you must be thirsty after your trip."

Eva drank the water gratefully and gave him back the glass so he could return it to the saloon.

"Now, Miss Eva," said Mr. Stonewall. "Where is it I'm taking you?"

Eva decided she'd better start at the beginning. She explained her entire circumstances starting with thirteen years ago when Sadie Lewis gave away her baby. Finally she told Mr. Stonewall the address on Holladay Street.

Mr. Stonewall let out a low whistle. He rubbed his forehead and frowned deeply. Then he sighed as if he was giving up on something he'd been trying to hold on to.

"Miss Eva," he said slowly, "if my Alice was still alive, we'd take you in and give you a home—I swear we would. But I've got just enough money to stay alive and hungry, and besides, it don't look proper for me to take you in with no wife to look after you." He shook his head. "I'll take you to this Holladay Street house. It's the only place you have to go to, I reckon.

And I'll just hope that since your mama cared enough about you to give you away that she'll take decent care of you now."

Cared *enough* to give her away?

"But," Mr. Stonewall continued, "if you're ever in trouble, I want you to come to me, you hear?"

Eva nodded.

"I mean it." He said it almost as if he were angry with her. *"You come to me if you need help."*

"I will," Eva said, though she couldn't understand why he seemed so agitated.

"Now, I'm going to show you where I live so you can find me anytime, day or night. I'm either in the train station or in my room or . . ." He seemed a little embarrassed. "Sometimes I stop in at that saloon back there where I got your water." Then he straightened up and added, "Sundays you'll find me at the African Baptist Church."

"Yes, sir," Eva said.

They walked down Blake Street to where the buildings lining the road were two- and three-story brick, some even taller, all crammed together with no space in between. Painted lettering on the outside of the buildings announced what was inside. There were cigar shops, liquor stores, grocers, butcher shops, saddle and harness makers, saloons, a bank, drugstores, milliners, barbershops. The street was a jumble of horse-drawn wagons and carriages, and down the center of the road, one white horse pulled a streetcar along smooth metal tracks. "I live right close to downtown," said Mr. Stonewall, raising his voice above the din of city noise.

Mr. Stonewall took her to his home, which was a basement room under a tobacco shop on Blake Street. It was cozy and neat, with a bed, washbasin, and big stove all in one room. "My Alice, she did like to bake," said Mr. Stonewall.

Eva promised she would remember where it was and would come to him if she needed anything. Next they cut over to Holladay Street and began to walk uptown. Soon they were out of the worst of the downtown crowds. Here there were still saloons and shops, but the street was quieter, with more homes and fewer businesses. Eva admired the buildings: brick two-story row houses with tall windows and wide wooden porches. She saw the women Mr. Stonewall had mentioned, lounging on porch swings and sitting at the windows, clothed in beautiful white dresses and flowered bonnets.

"Their fathers and husbands must be so wealthy!" Eva exclaimed.

Mr. Stonewall snorted, and Eva stared at him a moment. Did he begrudge these lovely women their good fortune?

After several blocks, Mr. Stonewall stopped in front of one of the richest-looking houses on the row. "This is 518," he said flatly.

"But . . ." Eva gazed, unbelieving, at the house. She shook her head. "How could she . . ." Anger rose inside her. "I thought she gave me away because she was *poor.*"

"Save your judgments, Miss Eva," said Mr. Stonewall. "I better leave you here before the marshal thinks I'm getting myself into trouble. Don't forget, you know where to find me. I'm only five, maybe six blocks away." He tipped his hat to her. "Us colored folks, we got to look out for one another. This here Colorado—it ain't Mississippi, but it ain't heaven neither." He hurried off down the street.

Eva stared at the 518 printed above the door. White lace curtains hung inside, making it hard for her to see the room beyond. "Mama Kate, Daddy Walter," she whispered, "I don't think this lady who gave me to you was telling the truth. Looks to me like she could've taken care of me fine, just didn't want to." She sighed. "I do wish you were both here to keep me. I can't see why she would want me now, and I don't want to go back to her anyway."

The white lace curtains fluttered, and Eva startled. Had someone seen her standing there, not knocking, talking to two dead people? She stepped forward quickly and knocked. Might as well get it over with.

The door swung open and a brown-skinned girl a little older than Eva stood and looked her up and down.

This must be—*had* to be—her sister. What was her name? "Pearl." Eva said it in a tight voice. So this was the sister who had grown up in this fancy house, while Eva had been given away on the street. Eva looked disdainfully at her starched, almost new gingham dress.

But the girl just narrowed her eyes. "Wait one minute," she said, then turned and marched away. Eva glanced around. In the sitting room to the left, a sofa and a pair of overstuffed chairs sat on a flowered rug. An ornately carved banister led up a flight of steps. Sunlight filtered in through the lace curtains on the windows. *That's all right,* she told her parents silently, feeling the need to apologize to them for her earlier thoughts. *I don't really wish I'd grown up here. I like our sod house, always with room for visitors, much better than this stuffy old place where nobody even gives you a proper hello.*

A tall white woman swept into the foyer and extended her hand to Eva. Her hair was auburn with streaks of gray, and she wore a long burgundy dress that made her look like a schoolmistress.

"Hello, I'm Miss Blanche Beaumont," she said, shaking Eva's hand. "The girls call me Miss B. Martha says you're a friend of Pearl's wanting employment."

Employment! Eva shook her head. "I'm happy to work, Miss, uh, Miss B. I know how to milk and garden and wash clothes and cook. My daddy even taught me how to shoe a horse. So don't get me wrong, but I'm not here looking for employment. I'm looking for my mother, Sadie Lewis, and my sister, Pearl. Sadie Lewis gave me away when I was born, and the folks who adopted me took right good care of me, but they're both dead now, so I had to come here."

The expression on Miss B's face changed quickly from a polite smile to bewilderment and then to outrage. "Martha!" she shouted, and the girl who had opened the door reappeared.

"Yes, Miss B," Martha answered, and cast a sidelong glance at Eva.

"Go fetch Sadie. And Pearl, too. They've been sleeping long enough." Miss B let her eyes settle on Eva with a look of such contempt that it made Eva's skin crawl.

Who was this Miss B? Why was *she* so angry at her? Eva began to back away toward the door. It had been a mistake to come here. She would go find Mrs. Santini and beg her husband to let her live with them. . . .

Martha came down the steps, followed by a woman and a teenage girl.

"Sadie," Miss B bellowed, "there is someone here to see you. Someone I'm sure you never intended for me to meet."

The woman stopped on the steps and stared blankly at Eva. For a moment, recognition dawned on her face, then a look of horror flashed. Her eyes rolled back and she collapsed, her head thudding loudly on the wooden steps as she landed. The teenage girl bent over her and cried, "Mama!"

Eva stared in shock and amazement. The woman passed out on the steps and her daughter, bending over her, were white.

Three more young white women came timidly down the steps. Two of them wore silk dressing gowns, and one, who was large, fleshy, and dark haired, had on only her bloomers and chemise. All of them were rubbing their eyes and yawning.

Sadie revived, and the two women in silk helped her into one of the overstuffed chairs. Miss B stood with her arms crossed in angry silence. The teenage girl—Eva realized *she* must be Pearl—squinted at Eva, studying her. Then she put her hands on her hips and addressed the woman in bloomers. "Lucille," she said. "She looks colored. Is she colored? You never told me she was colored."

The large woman's face lit up. "Is this Sadie's baby, all growed up? My Lord, you're beautiful, honey! I said she'd be beautiful, didn't I?" She came to Eva and wrapped her arms around her, nearly smothering her in huge soft breasts and the strong odor of armpits. She pulled back and looked at Eva up close. "What did they name you, honey? We never did know."

Eva peered at Lucille's face, with its layers of powder and rouge. She blinked. "Eva," she said.

"Eva," Lucille said with satisfaction. "Proper name for a proper girl. Look at her in her gingham and plain hat. Look at her, Sadie, ain't you proud?" Lucille grinned, and her two gold teeth flashed.

"Eva." Sadie said it softly.

Eva looked at Sadie, thinking she was about to say something to her. But she was merely trying out the name.

Of all the times Eva had tried to imagine her "light-skinned" mother, she had never imagined this! Sadie's skin was pale even for a white woman, and it had a pasty not-enough-sunshine look to it. Her nose was long and thin, her hair almost black, and smeared red lipstick made her mouth look uneven. She sat hunched over with her knees together in an ungainly pose that made Eva think of a praying mantis.

"How come nobody ever told me she was colored?" Pearl demanded. She was looking back and forth from Sadie to Lucille with a scowl almost as witchlike as Miss B's.

"Because a child could not be trusted with a secret that would have caused her mother to be thrown into the street." Miss B's voice was loud and harsh. "I do not allow colored to mix with my girls. And I do *not* allow working on the side. It's quite clear what happened here."

"Come on, Miss B," said Lucille, "it was all so long ago, and the girl is here for a nice visit. Let's have breakfast and show her some hospitality."

But no one moved.

"She is *not* here for a visit," Miss B said angrily. "She's here because her adoptive parents are dead."

Lucille stared dumbly at Miss B as if she hadn't understood. Pearl glared at Eva, and Sadie hung her head and whispered, "Oh, God."

Eva looked from one person to another. *Working on the side . . . , not allow colored to mix with my girls . . .* Miss B's words were like a puzzle coming together in Eva's mind even as she resisted the meaning of them. She shook her head. The preacher back home had talked about places he called "prisons of luxury" and "houses of sin," and when she'd asked, Mama Kate had explained what he meant. She backed toward the door. She had never, *ever* thought she would set foot in such a place. If she'd known what this house was, known what Sadie Lewis was, she never would have come. Without thinking of where she would go or what she would do, Eva swung the door open.

"Now you've gone and scared her off," she heard Lucille say. But she kept going, down the steps, glad to be breathing fresh air again.

"Eva!" Lucille called from the doorway. "Come on back. Miss B ain't as mean as she sounds sometimes."

Eva turned to see Lucille standing there in her underdrawers for all the world to see. *Lord,* she thought, *it is just as bad as the preacher said.*

"I—I can't stay in that house," Eva said. Would Lucille know what she meant? Take offense?

"But you came all this way," Lucille said sadly. "And I ain't seen you in so long—Sadie and Pearl neither. We're *glad* you're here, not sorry."

Hadn't seen her in so long? Was this the woman, the friend of Sadie's, who brought her, wrapped in a blanket, and gave her to Mama Kate and Daddy Walter? Eva felt a pang of longing, of wishing she could see that day so long ago, see both her parents alive again. She looked up at Lucille. *She held me when I was a baby,* she thought. *Can she be such an evil person?*

Lucille rubbed her bare arms. "Please come on in, Eva. I'm shivering here half naked."

Eva hesitated. She had nowhere else to go anyway. Mr. Stonewall had already said she couldn't stay with him, and she didn't know another soul in this city. She smelled biscuits baking and realized how hungry she was. She walked slowly up the steps.

Lucille put one arm around her. "Breakfast will be ready soon, honey. Bring your bag on upstairs. Pearl's bed is big enough for the two of you."

Eva didn't meet Pearl's eyes as she hurried past her to the stairs. Maybe Lucille was glad to have her here, but Pearl definitely was *not.*

● ● ●

"Mama Kate!" Eva whispered urgently. She sat on the bed, alone in Pearl's room. "You said you'd watch over me, so I hope you can hear me now. In case you weren't listening to all that just went on downstairs, this Sadie Lewis, she's a . . . well, she's the same thing as Mary Magdalene was, and I know the Lord forgave *her,* but that's because Mary Magdalene repented, and Sadie Lewis doesn't seem to have a mind to do any repenting, not as far as I can see." She hugged the carpetbag to her chest. "I know you wouldn't have sent me here if you'd known. I figure if you could come back to earth, you'd be pounding on the front door this minute, saying, 'Send Eva down here, I'm taking her home.'" The thought of Mama Kate at the front door made her so homesick she had to tighten her jaw against tears. "But you *can't* come back. So what should I do? Where else can I go?" She rocked back and forth on the bed, wishing that Mama Kate could answer her, tell her what to do, instead of only listening. "Well, if you got any ideas about where else I can go to live, I wouldn't mind hearing them if you can figure out a way to tell me."

A bell rang and Eva jumped. "All right, Mama Kate, that means breakfast is ready. And it's one o'clock in the afternoon— that gives you some idea of how mixed up things are in this house. But at least they're feeding me."

Breakfast was laid out on the dining room table and Lucille, Pearl, and the other two women, Ida and Ruby, were already serving themselves. Eva stopped a moment just to look at the food. It was as fancy and plentiful as a church picnic, with mounds of scrambled eggs, biscuits, thick slices of ham, a pitcher of milk, two bowls of jam, and coffee. A fat old German woman and Martha were still bringing plates and pitchers from the kitchen.

"Set down here, Eva," Lucille said with her mouth full of biscuit. "You're skinny as a broom handle."

Eva sat, and Ida passed her the ham. Ida had delicate, birdlike hands and round hazel eyes. Her hair curled softly in ringlets over her forehead and around her neck. "Take as much as you like," Ida said. "There's plenty."

Eva wondered briefly where Sadie was but then heard voices carrying down from upstairs: Sadie arguing with Miss B. She figured she might as well get a good meal in case Miss B was about to put her out on the street, so she loaded her plate with some of everything.

"You won't find a better cook than Gerta," said Ruby. "She'll fatten you up quick." Eva could see how Ruby got her name. Her hair was flaming red. She wore the front piled up on her head and the back flowing down, shiny as jewels. These ladies were kind and friendly—not at all the way she had imagined the "fallen women" from the preacher's sermons. Still, the thought of what they did for "work" made Eva's stomach roil.

After breakfast, instead of putting themselves to useful tasks, Lucille, Ida, and Ruby pulled out the bathtub and started boiling water for baths as if it were Saturday night instead of Thursday afternoon. The only person doing anything that looked like normal work was Martha, but when Eva tried to help her with changing the bed linens, she was shooed away and told to go help the girls with their baths. And all afternoon the doorbell rang, with deliveries of groceries, clean laundry, milk, ice, boxes of cigars, and bottles of liquor.

"Miss B says you can go to bed early tonight, seeing how you been through so much today," Pearl said with authority. She took a red silk dress out of her wardrobe, then unbuttoned her gingham dress in order to change. "*Don't* come over to my side of the bed—I'm only sharing because they say I got to—and *don't* touch my things while I'm working." She pulled the red dress over her head, and Eva noticed that it was short—to just below her knees. She also noticed that Pearl's legs were long and lanky, just like Sadie's and just like her own. *They're my blood mother and blood sister,* Eva thought, and frowned at the strangeness of it.

Pearl sat on the side of the bed and pulled on black silk stockings, clipping them into her garters. Then she plopped herself down at her dressing table, opened a jar of powder, and patted it onto her face with a round pink powder puff. "Miss B don't let me use rouge," she said. "She says I can't look like one of the girls if I ain't one of them." She turned and looked Eva in the eye. "Which I *ain't*." She closed the powder jar. "I dance in the dance hall, in case you're wondering." She pinned back her brown curls with two silver hair combs and completed her outfit by slipping her feet into a pair of soft red shoes. She turned to Eva with a flash of pride, a moment where it seemed as if she might say, "How do I look?" But her face quickly hardened into sternness, and she said, "I'll be tired when I come in, so don't be snoring or kicking or any such thing."

Eva sat stiffly on the bed, her arms crossed over her chest. *Lord, she's a bossy one,* she thought, and determined that she would snore, kick, *and* take up more than her half of the bed just to get Pearl back for being so sassy.

When Pearl had gone, Eva opened her carpetbag. She pulled out her nightclothes—the soft flannel gown, neatly patched with a square from Mama Kate's old everyday dress. She buried her nose in the flannel and breathed in. It had a nice soapy smell that reminded her of home. In this strange new house, the smells were all so different. There was smoke from the men's cigars—the older, well-dressed men Eva had caught a glimpse of in the evening just before she'd been ushered upstairs and out of sight. And there was the smell of the rouge and powders and perfumes the women wore, the stink of pee from the chamber pots no one seemed in a hurry to empty, and the odor of disinfectant mixed in with it all.

Eva pulled out her everyday dress from the carpetbag and held it up. The worn yellow calico had seemed quite nice to her just yesterday, but now it looked like a rag compared to the crisp gingham dresses and silk gowns these Denver women wore. She stuffed the old dress under the mattress. Tomorrow she'd throw it in the fire.

Eva carefully draped her Sunday dress and petticoat over a chair, checking to make sure the silver dollar was still in its hiding place. Then she pulled on her nightgown, combed out her braid, and crawled under the covers.

"Mama Kate," she whispered, "I want to tell you, there is one good thing about this place—maybe two. One, they got more food than Christmas, so you don't have to worry about me going hungry anymore like last winter. They had meat *and* eggs today, and it's not even Sunday! And two, the privy is the fanciest thing I've ever seen—it's got a porcelain seat, a basin of water, and plenty of newspaper to clean yourself with. I just thought you might be interested." Eva fluffed up her pillow and got comfortable. "And I promise I won't forget what you said about being proud and strong and not getting pushed anywhere I don't want to go." She yawned and could almost feel Mama Kate's gentle fingers stroking her hair. "Good night, Mama," she said.

Just before she fell asleep, she plopped one leg squarely onto Pearl's side of the bed.

When Eva awoke, the sun had climbed high into the sky. *Strange,* she thought, *it's the middle of the morning, and by the sound of it, I'm the only one awake.* She used the chamber pot, then poured water from the pitcher into the washbowl and washed the sleep out of her eyes. If she'd slept this late any day at home, Mama Kate would have been convinced she was sick— or lazy to the bone. But all night long, even until dawn, the house had been noisy with loud laughter, giggling, people tromping up and down the steps, and piano music wafting up from the dance hall downstairs. When Pearl had come to bed, she had awakened Eva by shoving her roughly to her own side of the double bed. Pearl now lay on her back, one arm flung over her head, snoring softly, with a smudge of face powder on the pillow next to her cheek.

So this was what Pearl had grown up with—gotten used to, even—her own mother and the other women in the house, day by day, selling their self-respect in exchange for plentiful food, fancy clothes, and a place to live. She wondered where Sadie and Lucille and the others had come from. What had made them choose this life instead of an honorable one? And how could they live with the shame of what they did to earn their keep?

Eva pulled on her clothes and walked quietly down the stairs. She wondered what she was supposed to do all morning while the rest of the house slept. From the kitchen she heard soft voices, and when she opened the door, she found Miss B, Martha, and the old cook, Gerta, sitting at the table, drinking coffee.

"You shouldn't get up so early," said Miss B. "You'll be working as late as Pearl soon." Then she addressed Gerta. "I'm putting her to work in the dance hall—she's certainly pretty enough."

Eva startled. Put her to work in the dance hall? *Dancing?* Until late at night? In a short dress, with powder on her face? "I don't know how to dance," she said flatly.

"Pearl will teach you," said Miss B with a wave of her hand.

"I'd rather help with cooking," Eva blurted out. "And I'm also good at washing or scrubbing floors. I can even clean the barn. . . . Do you have a barn?"

Gerta and Martha laughed at her. Miss B gave her a level gaze. "I already have a cook and a housekeeper. If you will live here, you will work *in the dance hall.* Now that's enough of your ridiculous talk."

Eva glared at Miss B. *Maybe I won't live here.* But even as she thought it, she slumped inside. Mr. Stonewall's words echoed in her mind: "It's the only place you have to go to. . . ."

"Martha," Miss B said, "go wake Pearl. Tell her to dress

properly. I'm sending these girls shopping." She glanced up at the clock. "Breakfast won't be for another four hours. Gerta, fix them some bread and butter."

Martha and Gerta obeyed immediately, and Eva wondered if anyone ever questioned Miss B.

Minutes later Pearl came into the kitchen, wearing a blue gingham dress, yawning, and looking very grumpy. "Miss B, why do I have to take her so *early*?" Pearl whined.

"Because respectable girls do their marketing in the morning, and I'll not have the town gossips saying I have underage girls working for me," Miss B snapped, then added under her breath, "I've already forked over enough money to the police this month, thank you."

Pearl grunted. She plopped down at the table and stared at the plate of bread and butter Gerta placed in front of her. "Then remember that silver brooch you said I needed for my green dress? The one in Reicheneker's store? I want it today instead of waiting," she said.

A silver brooch today just because she had to get up early? The girl had some nerve! Eva watched Miss B, eagerly anticipating her angry response.

"Oh, all right," Miss B said, only slightly annoyed. "Tell Mr. Reicheneker to put it on my account."

Eva let out a small cry of indignation. Pearl happily started in on her breakfast, and Miss B gave Eva a look that said, "Pay attention and you'll be buying jewels soon as well."

The morning was clear and cool, with a hint of autumn in the air. Pearl marched ahead of Eva, obviously not wanting to walk beside her, but not quite leaving her behind either.

"That Miss B," said Pearl, "she says, 'Don't let the customers see you wearing gingham—that's what they see at home all day,' and then she sends me shopping in gingham. What does she expect me to do if I see one of my customers? Run and hide?"

Eva walked at her own pace, and Pearl slowed down from time to time if she wanted an audience for her chattering. They left Holladay, cut across 19th to Larimer Street, and headed downtown, where the shops crowded side by side just like Eva had seen on Blake Street near Mr. Stonewall's. She read the colorful signs: BROWN'S BAKERY; L. A. MELBURN—BLACKSMITH; ROCKY MOUNTAIN NEWS PRINTING COMPANY; EATON, CYRUS & CO. WHOLESALE & RETAIL LIQUOR AND CIGARS. The air smelled of a mixture of baking bread, horse manure, cigar smoke, and printer's ink. And it seemed as if every third or fourth shop was a saloon.

The plank sidewalk took them over a narrow canal filled with foul-smelling water. Eva saw a workman come out of the German National Bank, lower a bucket into the canal, and use it to water a scrawny tree growing in front of the bank. A one-horse streetcar rumbled by on its tracks, with passengers' heads showing in all of the windows. Eva dodged the other pedestrians and the occasional pushcart of goods as they walked.

"Miss B says you can have a silk dress and dancing slippers made. And we can buy you hair combs," Pearl said, "and some better bloomers and camisoles than the ones you got."

Lord, Eva thought, *how does she know what kind of bloomers I've got?*

They came upon a group of men crouched in a circle on the sidewalk. One of them was throwing dice into the center of the circle. Pearl stopped, and Eva nearly collided with her. "Bet you can't tell which ones are visitors and have some money to spend," Pearl whispered to her.

Eva watched the group for a moment. Two were black men, three were white, and one was Mexican. All of them except the dice thrower wore the leather chaps, vest, and hat of a cowhand, and the smell of horses and sweat was strong in the air. Strangely, they all also looked clean shaven, as if they'd just gotten haircuts and shaves.

Pearl cupped her hand around Eva's ear and whispered, "I'll give you a hint. Look at the backs of their necks."

Eva did as Pearl said and saw that on the newly cleaned and trimmed necks of two of the men there was a small inverted *v* shaved into the hairline.

Eva raised her eyebrows and Pearl nodded, then grabbed Eva's hand and pulled her away, laughing.

"Is the *v* for 'visitor'?" Eva asked when they were out of earshot.

"More for 'victim,'" said Pearl. "The man with the dice sees that and knows they got some money to lose to him."

"Who shaved them that way?" Eva asked.

"The barbers," said Pearl. "They all do it. A cowhand or miner comes into town with two months of dirt and beard on his face and goes to the barbershop to get cleaned up. If he talks like he's brought in a prize herd or struck a lode of silver, the barber just kind of advertises that fact for anyone who might be interested."

"But that's not fair," Eva objected.

"You don't get fed in this town by being fair," said Pearl.

She marched off ahead of Eva again.

At Reicheneker's store, Pearl pointed to a beautiful brooch of silver filigree woven into the shape of a flower. Mr. Reicheneker took it out of its case, and Pearl fastened it onto her dress. "Just put it on Miss B's account," Pearl ordered.

Mr. Reicheneker nodded but raised one eyebrow and gave them a disapproving stare. Eva felt his eyes on her back as they left the store.

At the dressmaker's, Pearl told Mrs. O'Regan, the seamstress,

what color Eva wanted (royal blue), what style (short, to just below the knees, with a new petticoat the same length), and that the
dress, petticoat, and cloth dancing shoes had to be ready in a few
days since she didn't want Eva ruining all of her dresses, which
she'd have to borrow until her own was ready. Mrs. O'Regan took
out a tape and set about measuring Eva's hips, waist, bust, arms,
and length from shoulders to knees. Then she argued with Pearl
that she really should make the hemline longer.

"Miss B is paying, and that's how short she wants it," Pearl
said firmly.

"Miss B should be hung—you know that, don't you?" said
Mrs. O'Regan.

Pearl rolled her eyes. "We're only just dancing," she said.

Mrs. O'Regan scowled. "Dancing. School is where you
ought to be. Somebody should call the authorities. Maybe it's
me should be hung, making these dresses when I know you girls
are only children." Suddenly she fixed Eva with her eyes. "How
do you come to be working for Miss B, anyway?"

Did she really want to hear the whole story? Eva thought not.

Pearl crossed her arms and lifted her chin. "She don't have
to tell you a thing. Miss B will send Martha to pick up that dress
in a couple of days." She grabbed Eva by the arm and yanked her
out the door.

The hair combs and new underclothes were forgotten as
Pearl led Eva home in much the same way as she'd led her to the

shop, marching on ahead and talking most of the way. "Shoot, that woman is nosy and throwing her opinions around as if I cared. School? I'll give her school. I went to that Arapahoe school for a while when it first opened. I never learned *nothing* there, except how those 'proper' children can punch *hard* when they think they're better than you. That's how I lost this tooth." She slowed long enough for Eva to catch up and take a look at the gap in her mouth. "And black eyes—I got two in one week once. *School.* Shoot."

She took off ahead of Eva again. "And her talking about calling the authorities and complaining about making our dresses, like she's lowering herself to do the job. Only reason she even got this job is her brother is one of our regular customers. Her brother the *policeman.*" Pearl stopped short and pointed her finger at Eva. "When I was six years old, a lady asked me where I lived and I said, 'At the police station.' Do you know why?"

Eva shook her head.

"Because there was so many policemen in their uniforms coming and going from Miss B's place, I figured it must be the police station. They're either there to pick up their bribe money, there to act like they're checking up on things, or there doing business like everybody else. The *authorities.* Shoot."

It was nearly noon, and they passed an eating house with men, most of whom looked like miners and cowhands, lined up outside. A sign said CAMELLERI'S and, in smaller letters, ALL MEALS PREPARED BY MRS. CAMELLERI HERSELF.

The men hooted at them, and Pearl flounced as she walked by. Eva hoped they were hooting at Pearl and not her, but she blushed anyway. "Look at them," said Pearl, "all lined up in the street just to get a meal cooked by a woman. They must eat some *bad* cooking on their cow drives and up in their mining camps!"

They passed two more eating houses—John Newby's and Henry Bredenburg's—with no lines out front. Eva guessed there might be men doing the cooking at those places. When they arrived at 518 Holladay Street, Pearl stomped up the steps, entered, and closed the door in Eva's face. Eva put her hand on the doorknob but didn't open it. Out in the world, at Mrs. O'Regan's dress shop, Pearl had presented a united front. But here at what was meant to be Eva's new home, she was shut out, still an intruder. She sat down on the front stoop and rested her chin in one hand. The smell of fresh biscuits and frying bacon had wafted out when Pearl opened the door, and it still hung in the air. The sky was the same bright blue as it had always been on late summer days at home.

"Mama Kate," Eva whispered. "Looks like I'm going to be doing some dancing. I suppose it'll be like the time I waltzed with Daddy Walter at the country fair." She thought a moment. Should she tell Mama Kate about the short dress? Oh, heck, she'd see it soon enough. "I don't think you'll like my new dress very much. But I was thinking about how we used to tuck up our skirts and go wading in the Big Sandy Creek on real hot days, and you'd say if the good Lord meant for our legs to be covered every single minute of every day, then he'd have wrapped us in wool before we were born. Remember? So I hope you understand." A breeze blew and lifted the hem of Eva's dress slightly. "*Do* you understand, Mama Kate?" She smiled, hoping the breeze had been her answer.

"So it looks like I'll be able to pay my way with this dancing, and that's a good thing, right? Pearl does it, and it looks like she has fun getting dressed up for it." She sighed. "Mama Kate? I hope I'm still making you glad." She stood, opened the door, and walked inside.

"Eva, get on in here, food's getting cold," Lucille called from the dining room as Eva walked inside.

"She ate as much as a horse last night at supper. She don't need no breakfast," said Pearl.

"Oh yes she does—here's a plate, honey." Lucille handed Eva a dish already piled with bacon, sausages, and biscuits. There was a newcomer at the table: Sadie had finally joined them for a meal. Only Miss B was absent.

Taking her place, Eva studied Sadie out of the corner of her eye. She wasn't graceful or pretty. Gawky, that's what she was, all elbows and knees, with her black hair in sharp contrast to her pallid skin. Was the woman ever going to talk to her? she wondered. Explain things to her, tell her who her father was?

Lucille interrupted her thoughts. "You were so tired from your trip yesterday, we didn't get to hear a thing," she said. "Tell us about yourself—the Wilkinses, they were colored folks, right?"

Eva nodded. "Yes, ma'am."

"I remember them now," said Lucille. "I was the one that found them. We knew you was colored, so I figured I'd better find colored folks for you to grow up with."

Eva glanced at Sadie to see how she'd react to this statement. But her eyes had a strange, red-rimmed, vacant look that made Eva so uneasy she looked away.

"You are a beauty, though," Lucille continued. "Better teach her the hat pin trick, huh, Pearl?" She shoved Pearl's shoulder as she took a drink of milk, and Pearl snorted and sprayed milk onto the tablecloth.

"*Lucille!*" Pearl whined, and wiped her chin with her hand. "I'll teach her what she needs to know," she said, annoyed.

Martha came into the dining room with a plate of scrambled eggs, and the women passed it around the table. Eva took a large serving. If she was going to be made to dance for her keep, bossed around by Pearl, and ignored by her mother, she was at least going to enjoy eating the most plentiful meals she'd ever seen in her life.

"I told you she'd grow up to be a beauty, remember, Sadie?" Lucille asked.

But Sadie's head drooped, and her eyes were half closed. She hadn't touched the food.

Ida, who was sitting next to Sadie, tried to prod her to life. "She probably didn't get much sleep last night," said Ida, laughing nervously.

When Sadie barely roused, there was an uncomfortable silence at the table.

At that moment Miss B stormed in. "For Chrissake, the laudanum is half gone—" She took one look at Sadie and pounced.

She pulled Sadie up by her shoulders, and her head fell to one side. "Fetch Doc Stevens," she cried. "Help me get her upstairs."

Lucille, Ruby, and Miss B hoisted Sadie out of her chair. Pearl started to cry, and Ida ran out the front door, calling, "I'll fetch the doctor!"

As the women moved up the steps, Eva heard Miss B grunt under Sadie's weight, then say, "Get the chamber pot ready. I'll stick my finger down her throat."

The sounds of retching upstairs made the pile of scrambled eggs on Eva's plate look disgusting. Pearl had gone pale and was shaking with sobs.

"What—what's wrong with her?" Eva asked.

Pearl looked up at her, glaring hatred. "This is your fault!" She spat out the words. "You almost killed her once, and now you're back to finish her off. Why couldn't you have just stayed away?!" Pearl shoved her dishes onto the carpet and ran from the room.

Doc Stevens rested his large hand on Pearl's shoulder. "She's going to pull through, Pearl. Believe me, I'd know it if she was too far gone. I lost two girls last week on this street, one from laudanum overdose and one, God help me, swallowed half a box of Rough on Rats."

Pearl looked up at him, her eyes swollen and her face shiny with tears.

"But your mama, she's just sleeping peacefully now. Miss B

got to her fast enough and knew just what to do—you can thank her for that," he said.

Pearl nodded.

Eva wondered if Pearl was right—if it *was* her fault that Sadie had taken the laudanum, that just by showing up she'd made Sadie want to die. But how could she have known about Miss B and the rules and all the rest? And what would she do now if Sadie did die? She would, truly, have no place to go.

Miss B and the doctor went into the foyer and spoke in hushed tones. Eva saw Miss B count out cash into his hand and lead him to the door. Then Miss B returned and put her arm around Pearl.

"No dancing tonight, Pearl. I'm closing the dance hall for now. You can sit up with your mother if you'd like."

Pearl sniffed and walked slowly up the steps, her shoulders sagging.

"Eva," Miss B said, "I know she's your mother, too, but—"

"I don't need to sit with her," Eva said quickly. "I believe Doc Stevens that she'll be fine."

"Good," said Miss B. "Get Lucille to show you the dance hall, explain to you how we do things. That way you'll be ready when we open again in a few days."

"Yes, ma'am," said Eva, glad to be given something to do.

The "dance hall" was just a back parlor room with a scuffed-up wooden floor, heavy red drapes, a few tables and chairs for card playing and gambling, a piano shoved up against one wall, and a bar in front of shelves filled with bottles of whiskey. It smelled of stale smoke and seemed strangely quiet sitting here empty in the midafternoon.

"It's all pretty simple," Lucille said. "A boy asks you to dance, and you say yes, and he pays twenty-five cents to Gus— he's the bartender. He'll give it to Miss B, and she'll divvy it up with you later."

Eva nodded. She ran her hand along the smooth edge of the bar and imagined the room filled with people and music.

"Anyway," Lucille continued, "after you dance, you say, 'My, that makes a body thirsty!' and try to get him to buy you a drink—but not a ten-cent beer. Miss B don't allow us girls to drink alcohol. What you want to order is one of them fancy cocktails, costs a dollar."

"A dollar!" Eva exclaimed. "What on earth do they put in them to make them cost a dollar? Gold dust?"

Lucille laughed. "No, honey, all they are is water colored with a little saffron and maybe some sugar if Gus is in a good mood. But fifty cents of that dollar goes to *you*—that's why you try to get the fella to buy it for you. And you be nice and talk to him while you sip it."

Eva's eyes bugged out. Fifty cents was enough to buy a whole sack of cornmeal. And she could make more than that in one evening? She and Mama Kate wouldn't ever have gone hungry if she could have started this job a long time ago.

A shaft of sunlight filtered in between the red drapes, and dust danced in the light. Eva decided to venture a question. "Lucille?"

"What, honey?"

"Did I live in this house for a while before Sadie gave me away?"

"Only for a day or so," said Lucille. "Just until I could find a home for you."

"That's when you found Mama Kate and Daddy Walter?" Eva liked imagining her parents walking the streets of Denver, the same streets she had now walked.

"That's right. When you came out, we knew right away who the daddy was, and it was just what Sadie was afraid of, too. She met that colored boy during the summer. Miss B took all us girls and a tent up into the mountains to have a little vacation from the Denver heat and work a couple of mining towns while we was up there. That boy took to your mama something powerful. Didn't want to hear that Miss B didn't allow colored. So he offered to pay your mama on the side if she'd sneak out with him. She needed the money, what with Pearl always needing a new bunting or a visit to the doctor, and she liked the boy well enough, too, said he was a gentleman, so she agreed."

Eva mused, *So that's where the spark of my life began, up in those monstrous gray mountains, in the summertime....*

Lucille sat down on one of the high bar stools, her large rump spilling over the edges, and leaned her elbows on the bar. "Sadie knew Miss B would be furious when she found out she was having *another* baby and would most likely call in the doctor to get rid of it. But we'd lost a girl a few months before that way—bled to death right in that room where you and Pearl sleep. Sadie took it hard, and it scared her, too. So she wore corsets to hide the baby—you—until it was too late to call in the doctor. And Sadie was *positive* Miss B would throw her out if she found out she'd been working on the side. One thing Miss B insists on is that we girls are honest—no robbing the customers, no cheating the house. That's why there's no bars on the windows the way there are in some houses. Every girl here knows if she lets a boy sneak in a window, she'll be thrown out in the street the next day.

"So when you arrived and we could see in your sweet face who the daddy was, Sadie was all in a panic. We was going to give you away no matter who the father turned out to be, but as it was, we had Ruby pretend to have fits in order to keep Miss B busy, and I sneaked you out without Miss B ever laying eyes on you."

Lucille's expression turned serious, and her eyes seemed to look back in time. "Doc Stevens said we'd a done better to keep you for a few days, that Sadie wouldn't have bled so bad if she'd been able to suckle you for longer." Lucille looked at Eva, and it took a moment for her eyes to focus. "We almost lost her," she said quietly.

So that's what Pearl meant about Eva—or her birth, any-way—nearly killing their mother. Pearl was only a toddler at the time, but surely she must have heard about it later when she was old enough to understand. "But why does Pearl think that I'm trying to kill Sadie *now*?" she asked.

Lucille shook her head. "That Pearl is just jealous. She thinks your mama took the laudanum because you're here. But girls do that all the time. Miss B lets us take a little every day if we want—it makes our work go by easier. But for some girls, espe-cially if they get to thinking about their relatives and families back home, it gets to be too much, and they want to swallow the whole bottle of the stuff. Don't you worry about Sadie. You showing up has been a shock, but she'll get over it, you'll see."

Eva nodded. She wondered what Pearl could possibly find to be jealous of since Sadie hadn't even said two words to Eva since she'd arrived. She was also curious about the family back home Sadie might still think about sometimes, the relatives that were her relatives, too. She decided that as soon as Sadie was well, she would ask her about them.

The bell rang, signaling that hot water was ready for after-noon baths, and Lucille rose to leave. "You'll do fine dancing, honey," she said with a quick smile that seemed to lack any joy behind it. "You'll get used to it."

Eva stayed in the quiet dance hall after Lucille left. She picked at a splintered bit of wood on a bar stool and looked around the dimly lit room. She remembered that breezy afternoon at the country fair, with Mr. Baytop on banjo and Charlie Scott on fiddle, when Daddy Walter had asked her for a waltz as if he were asking a princess to dance. She had laughed as he guided her over the lumpy grass because she really didn't know how to waltz and she was making lots of mistakes. But he still treated her as if she was the most wonderful dancer in the world. She remembered his smiling face, his one hand light at her waist, his other hand holding hers firmly. There couldn't be anything so hard to get used to about this job of dancing, she decided.

She peeked at the door to make sure no one was watching. Then, imagining a breezy spring day on the prairie and imagining Daddy Walter as her partner, she stepped out onto the dance floor and whirled to the music of a banjo and fiddle being played under the wide Colorado sky.

The dance hall stayed closed for a few days so that Pearl could tend to Sadie while she got on her feet again. Lucille, Ida, and Ruby still worked nights, and Martha and Gerta were busy with household chores and receiving deliveries of groceries and liquor. Eva washed her stockings and underclothes and hung them to dry, pulled her everyday dress out of its hiding place under the mattress and burned it in the stove while no one was looking, and had her Saturday bath along with the girls in the kitchen. After that, she had nothing to do.

She went upstairs and found Lucille in her bedroom, sitting at her dressing table. "Lucille, can I go to school here when it starts?" Eva asked.

Lucille took a contraption out of her kerosene lamp: long metal tongs with a wooden handle. She grasped a lock of her hair with the tongs, twisted until the hair was wrapped tightly, and held it like that for a moment. When she released the tongs, Eva was astounded: the hair was curled into a beautiful ringlet. Lucille put the tongs back into the lamp to heat up again, and Eva stood with her mouth open.

"You never seen a curling iron before, honey?" Lucille asked.

Eva shook her head.

"Want me to do yours?" Lucille took the hot curling iron out of the lamp and pointed it toward Eva's locks. But the smell of burning hair made Eva hesitate. "Um, no thank you," she said. "But do you think I can go to school when it starts up?"

Lucille pursed her lips and went back to work on her hair. "That Miss B, she thinks nobody needs any schooling once they're old enough to work. She won't want to be paying for your books or seeing you act tired from getting up early for school after dancing half the night. I'm sorry, honey, but I think you better hush about school."

Eva frowned but nodded that she understood. She watched Lucille produce a few more ringlets with the curling iron and then went back to her own room. "Mama Kate," she said. "I asked about school, but it sounds like I won't be going. I know you wanted me to keep on with my schooling even though I'm plenty old enough to work. I'm real sorry to disappoint you." She sighed. "Maybe I'll get back to school someday."

No school, no household chores, nothing to do. Eva felt jittery with idleness. There weren't even any books in the house.

On Sunday morning, with most everyone still asleep, Eva found Miss B in the sitting room at her desk, recording sums in her accounting book. "Miss B," Eva ventured, "I'd like to visit a . . . friend of mine today."

Miss B raised her eyebrows, as if to question how Eva might

have a friend here in Denver. "Where does this friend live?" she demanded.

"On Blake Street, below Snider's pipe and tobacco store," Eva answered.

"And she invited you?" Miss B asked.

"Yes, *he* invited me." Then she explained quickly, "He's old— an old man. He helped me find your house the day I arrived and told me what church he goes to. I thought I'd join him there."

Miss B dipped her quill pen in the ink. "All right, then. If you're not back by five, we'll have supper without you."

Eva skipped upstairs to get her hat, being careful not to wake Pearl. She found her way easily from Holladay Street to Blake Street. If she ever needed to know what direction she was walking, she only needed to spot the mountains to know which way was west. Today the morning sun had turned them a soft purple. She was getting used to the mountains being there, but she tried not to look at them if she could help it. They still seemed eerie.

As Eva walked toward Mr. Stonewall's, she noticed that the streets were unusually quiet. Was this because Sunday was a day to refrain from gambling and drinking? she wondered. Or was it because everyone was still asleep from Saturday night rabble-rousing?

She passed a saloon and saw that the doors were open. From

inside she heard voices—children's voices—so she peeked in. Two young boys in scruffy overalls and tattered shirts crouched on the floor.

"Hoo-ee! That's a big one!" One of the boys held up a long straight pin with something very small and shiny stuck to the end. He shook his stringy blond hair out of his eyes.

"That'll buy you new shoes," said the other boy, who was smaller and quite freckled. "Or maybe a horse!"

They both set to giggling. The blond boy carefully dipped his pin, with its precious cargo, into a leather pouch. The freckled boy bent over the floor, peering between the floorboards and picking at the crevices with his own straight pin.

"Pssst. What are you doing?" Eva asked.

The boys glanced up at her, then went right back to work. "This is our territory. You got to go someplace else," said the one who'd found the shiny treasure.

"The owner's a friend of my uncle," said the smaller boy. "All the gold dust falls in here belongs to *us*."

"How does the gold dust fall?" Eva asked. She was curious enough to keep bothering them.

The blond boy sat back on his haunches. "Don't you know *nothing*?"

"She's just a dumb girl," mumbled the other boy, still intent on his work.

Eva narrowed her eyes at them. "I guess you must be too

stupid to know how the dust falls, and that's why you can't answer my question."

The freckled boy scrambled to his feet. "I am *not* stupid! The dust falls when the miners open their pouches to pay for whiskey or gambling or for a girl and they spill some."

Eva nodded and smiled slightly, the way her teacher at school used to do when a student gave the right answer. "Very good," she said. Her eyes had adjusted to the dim light inside the saloon, and she suddenly became aware of a huge cat's head mounted, scowling, above the bar. She took a step back, staring. It was ten times the size of a normal cat, with thick folds of tawny pelt and bared yellow fangs.

"You like that?" the freckled boy asked. "My uncle shot that mountain lion right after it killed a man."

Eva shivered involuntarily.

"I think she likes it," said the blond boy. "The bartender keeps one of its feet behind the bar—claws and all. Here, I'll show you." He ducked behind the bar, but Eva turned quickly and was out the saloon door before the severed mountain lion foot could be produced. She heard the boys laughing as she walked down the street.

When Eva reached Mr. Stonewall's home, she stepped down to his door and knocked. She heard shuffling from inside and hoped she hadn't awakened him too early. Mr. Stonewall opened the door and blinked in the bright sunshine, standing barefoot and in his long underwear. "Miss Eva!" he exclaimed, his voice still rusty with sleep. "Lord, I been thinking about you every day." His face went suddenly serious. "Is something wrong? Is that why you come?"

Eva shook her head. "No, I'm fine. I came for a visit and was hoping you'd take me to church with you."

Mr. Stonewall nodded happily. "Wait right there while I make myself decent."

He shut the door, and Eva raised her face, eyes closed, to the morning sun. He was glad to see her. That felt good enough to grin about.

"Services don't start till noon," Mr. Stonewall told her when they were settled at the little round table next to the stove, with mugs of hot tea and day-old bread with jam. "That way the preacher hopes to get some of the riffraff who stay up all night and sleep late." He was dressed in his Sunday suit, but his shirt collar was still undone.

"Like *you*?" Eva teased.

Mr. Stonewall gave her a worried look. "They're not turning you smart-mouthed already, are they?"

Eva cast her eyes down, ashamed. Was she already taking on some of Pearl's disrespectful ways? "I'm sorry, Mr. Stonewall, I didn't mean to be fresh."

"No need to apologize." He patted her hand. "You're right.

It must be near eleven." He yawned. "But tell me, how are they treating you at that place?"

Between sips of strong tea and bites of jellied bread, Eva told him about Sadie and Pearl, Miss B, Lucille, and the other women and the events of the last few days; some of the events, not all of them. Why worry him with talk of short dresses and dancing? When she was done, Mr. Stonewall looked stern.

"That's no place for a child to grow up, with whiskey at one end of the house and laudanum at the other." He shook his head. Then he brightened. "I reckon you'll be starting school soon. That new Arapahoe school is right near you, takes white and colored."

Eva squirmed. She'd been able to leave things out of her story, but she didn't want to outright lie to Mr. Stonewall. "Maybe . . . I haven't talked to Miss B about it yet." She stood. "Isn't it time to go?"

Mr. Stonewall slowly wiped crumbs from his lips. "You didn't forget what I told you about coming to me for help, did you?" He eyed her as if he saw something murky behind her carefully worded answers.

"No, sir, I didn't forget," said Eva.

"Good." He put down his napkin. "Now one more thing. When we go to church, you'll meet some of the most respectable black folks in Denver. We're not going to tell them you live on Holladay Street. No sense starting tongues wagging for no reason, you understand?"

Eva nodded, grateful that he had thought of this. She didn't want anyone at church to think less of her because of where she lived.

Mr. Stonewall put on his tie, brushed the shoulders of his suit jacket, and stood up tall. He looked regal despite the worn, faded fabric.

Eva smoothed the front of her Sunday dress and squared her shoulders. "Do we look respectable?" she asked.

"Mighty respectable." Mr. Stonewall held out his arm. She took it, and together they emerged from the tiny basement room into the warm sunshine and walked arm in arm toward church.

"Look at this nice sunny morning and us going to church." Mr. Stonewall hummed with satisfaction. "Years ago, when I first came to Denver, you could hardly find a church for Sunday morning, but you *could* find blood on the sidewalk in front of the barrooms where they'd dragged out the poor wretch who'd got shot the night before. Back in those days I heard more shots fired on a Saturday night than in a month of good hunting."

Eva stopped walking. "I heard shots last night," she said weakly. "I thought somebody was night hunting."

Mr. Stonewall pulled her along. "Miss Eva, you're living in

the city now. Ain't no night hunting around here—unless that's what you call shooting the fellow who cheats you at poker!" He laughed until he saw the stricken look on Eva's face. "Come on now, you got nothing to worry about. Most of the shooting is over gambling. Just don't go playing blackjack," he said.

The African Baptist Church was a simple wooden structure, neatly painted white and nestled between 20th and 21st on Arapahoe Street. When they arrived, parishioners stood out front, chatting in small groups, dressed in their Sunday best. A tall woman in a sweeping peach-colored dress and feathered hat walked right up to Eva and Mr. Stonewall.

"Brother Stonewall, who is this pretty young lady you brought with you today?" she asked, and smiled warmly at Eva.

"This is my niece, and she's here visiting. Miss Eva, this is Sister Boyd."

"I didn't know you had a niece!" Mrs. Boyd exclaimed.

Mr. Stonewall cocked his head. "Do I have to tell you everything?"

Mrs. Boyd laughed. A small girl with sticking-out braids came over shyly, took Eva's hand, and beamed up at her.

"Carrie, this is Eva," said Mrs. Boyd. "Can you say, 'Welcome to our church'?"

"Welcome to our church," the little girl said in a high, sweet voice.

Eva was then introduced to more people than she could count: Deacon Riley, Reverend Norrid, Sister Armstrong, looking like springtime in a bright flower-print dress, and Brother Sanderline, who teased Mr. Stonewall about his hair being too long and said he expected to see him at his barbershop right soon.

When the church bells rang, Mrs. Boyd slipped her arm through Eva's and said, "Come on and sit with me."

Inside, the church had the same feeling of peaceful stillness she remembered from church back home. She and Mama Kate and Daddy Walter had always sat in the back, not wanting to ruffle the feathers of any townspeople who thought that's where they belonged. But here, Mrs. Boyd led her right up front.

The peaceful stillness was interrupted when two young boys came bursting in the door in a game of chase. Mrs. Boyd put a stop to that in a hurry. "*Why* are you ripping and running through the Lord's house? Have some respect." The boys instantly calmed down and walked quietly to a pew. But when Eva glanced back at them, they were poking each other.

The singing began as humming until they raised a hymn, and "My Lord, What a Morning" filled the tiny church with an ocean of voices. When the music had died down, Reverend Norrid stepped up to the pulpit and began his sermon. Eva tried to keep her mind from wandering but soon found that instead of listening, she was having a bit of an argument with

God. Not that God was arguing back—just that she felt the need to explain herself.

I couldn't tell him—you see how he worries so. I didn't want to upset him with talk of the dance hall. And Mama Kate will understand. She said herself that You would have wrapped us in wool like the sheep if You wanted our legs covered all the time. What choice do I have anyway? I don't see You sending my aunt Linnie to come get me. Anyway, I saw Pearl getting ready to go dance, and it looked fun. I'll wear powder on my face, and my dress will be blue. . . .

After a time, the congregation began to sing again, and Eva joined her voice with theirs.

After services there was eating and talking and laughing, with Mr. Stonewall telling stories and three of the older ladies hanging on his every word. Eva breathed easy, feeling like herself for the first time in days.

On their way walking back home, Eva asked, "Do you think they'll believe you if every week you tell them I'm visiting?"

"You coming next Sunday, too?" Mr. Stonewall asked happily. "Don't worry about those folks—they been through hard times, almost all of them, and there's nobody who will turn you out or ask too many questions once they know you."

They parted ways at Holladay Street. Eva understood Mr. Stonewall's embarrassment about walking down her street and assured him that she could get herself back safely.

The Eaton, Cyrus & Co. liquor store truck was already

making deliveries. Eva guessed that the drinking, gambling, and carousing would all begin again in just a few hours. But she wanted to remain a little longer in the warm glow of the African Baptist Church. As she walked, she sang softly, "Steal away, steal away, steal away to Jesus. Steal away, steal away home. . . ."

Eva and Pearl had been going to bed at different times and getting up at different times, so although they shared a bed, it had been easy to avoid each other. Tonight, however, they found themselves undressing at the same time. Eva decided to broach the awkward silence.

"You still think she took the laudanum because of me?" she asked. She didn't know whether to say "Sadie," "your mama," or "our mama," so she just said "she."

"Yes," came Pearl's one-word answer. There was a tiredness, a worn-out-ness in her voice that Eva had never heard before.

"You still mad at me about it?" Eva asked.

"Yes," said Pearl. Then she added, "Miss B says she's got to open the dance hall soon or she'll go broke. And Mama has to start working again, too."

Eva turned out the kerosene lamp and they both lay down in the darkness.

"Where did you go today?" Pearl asked. She sounded friend-lier, as if having the opportunity to say she was mad had made her less mad.

"To church," Eva answered.

Pearl snorted. "What the hell did you do that for?"

Eva widened her eyes at Pearl's choice of words, then smiled. It was good to hear Pearl's feistiness again. "I thought it would be pleasant, and it was," she answered.

They were quiet for a while. Then Pearl spoke. "I never been to church. Ain't no church around would have us."

Eva was struck by the harshness of this. Of course, no respectable woman would be willing to share a pew with Sadie or Lucille or the likes of them. Lucille had told her that the opera houses didn't even let the girls go to shows because if they did, patrons would demand their money back rather than sit next to a fallen woman.

She could take Pearl with her next week, she thought. Pearl wasn't a fallen woman. She smiled to think of Pearl's white face among all those dark ones, singing "Go Down, Moses." Mr. Stonewall had said that most people there had been through hard times and would not be quick to judge. She would introduce Pearl as her sister, and folks would be nice.

"You could come with me if you want to—" she began.

"*No* thank you," Pearl shot back.

Eva guessed that Pearl probably liked the thought of church about as much as she liked the thought of school.

"Tomorrow I got to teach you to dance—Miss B says," Pearl said. She yawned and rolled over with her back to Eva.

Eva fell asleep imagining collecting twenty-five-cent and fifty-cent pieces and dropping them into her dress pocket.

● ● ●

The confrontation had been inevitable, Eva realized. They met quite by accident out behind the house in the crisp cold of early morning, with Eva at the water pump as Sadie emerged from the privy.

At first they simply looked at each other, and all of Eva's questions tumbled through her mind. *What was my father's name? Did you love him? Do I have grandparents somewhere? Aunts, uncles, cousins? How did you end up working here? Isn't it awful, what you have to do upstairs? How can you stand it? Why didn't you want thank-you letters from me at Christmastime? Why did you take the laudanum—was it that terrible to see me again? Did you miss me when you gave me away? Don't you care that I'm here now?* But instead of speaking, she froze, her hand on the pump, her mouth open and no words coming.

Sadie looked so young with her face clean of makeup and her dark hair an uncombed tumble. Eva realized that she *was* young, much younger than Mama Kate had been, maybe not even thirty yet.

"I know what you're thinking." Sadie broke the silence, her voice hard.

Eva startled. Did she really know all of her questions?

"You come in here with your nose in the air, saying, 'I'll help cook and clean' and going to church like you're the only one ever heard of morals." She raked hair away from her face. "You think I'm no good, that I'm nothing but trash compared to that colored woman who raised you."

Eva straightened up, ready to object, ready to tell her, "I never said you were trash!" but Sadie kept going, kept talking, and there was no room to object.

"*You* just try it—try it for two days on your own in Denver, with a ma and pa back home who are too sad to work, with two brothers just buried and a baby sister who'll go hungry if you don't send money. You try it when you're hungry and there ain't no job for an ignorant farm girl in a worn-out dress. Think you could do better, Miss High and Mighty?"

Eva shook her head almost imperceptibly.

"No, you couldn't. So I don't want to hear no guff about *what I am*, you understand? It's not my fault those people up and died. I did the best I could, sending you away. I didn't want you here. But now that you're here, remember it's because of me"—she pointed to her own chest in a violent jerk—"that you're working *down*stairs instead of *up*stairs." Sadie stood there, opening and closing her fists, her face flushed.

"I never said you were no good," Eva said quietly.

Sadie's shoulders relaxed a bit, as if Eva had taken a weight off them.

"Why didn't you want thank-you letters from me for the

Christmas money?" Eva asked. It certainly wasn't the most important question, just the one she most had the courage to ask.

Sadie frowned as if she didn't understand.

"The letter, the one you wrote that first Christmas, it said not to write back. I would have written to thank you. . . ."

Sadie collapsed like a rag doll, slumping down to sit on an overturned bucket. "You saw the letter?" she asked quietly. "She saved it all those years?" She rubbed her forehead with two fingers. "I thought of you on that farm, figured you were growing up the way I did, with a ma and pa and good hard daytime work." She looked up at Eva, her eyes sad. "I didn't want you to ever come here, didn't want you to even know where I lived. I wanted you to stay . . . innocent."

Before Eva could ask more questions, Sadie straightened herself up, seemed to harden over the softness she had just shown. "Well." She rubbed her hands together to warm them. "What's done is done, and no use crying over it." She walked briskly into the house.

"Step when I step," said Pearl. "It'll be easier with the Professor playing piano, but this is how we got to do it now."

Sun streamed in the sitting room windows, and Ruby, Ida, and Lucille lounged on the overstuffed chairs to watch the dance lesson. Eva concentrated on her feet. One-two-three, one-two-three. Pearl said the waltz was the easiest, so that's how they'd start.

"You're doing good!" Lucille applauded as the girls whirled gracefully around the room.

Pearl's hand, firm on Eva's waist, guided her. The new soft blue shoes had arrived that morning, along with the dress, and in them her feet seemed to glide over the rug.

Pearl stopped abruptly. "Now let's do the polka. That's almost the same count, only faster and with a hop. Like this."

Eva was dragged into a sloppy polka, feeling like a horse pulled into a canter even before she was trotting. She tried to keep up but stepped on Pearl's feet at least twice.

"Pearl, she needs music," Ida complained.

Pearl stopped, out of breath and annoyed. "Where am I going to get music this time of day?" she demanded.

Lucille started clapping in rhythm and belting out "Shoo, Fly, Don't Bother Me." She was sorrowfully off-key, but when Ida and Ruby joined in, it actually sounded reasonably good.

Pearl looked at Eva. "Can you hear it? One-two-three-hop, one-two-three-hop." Then she whisked Eva into the lively circles of a fast polka. Eva stepped to the beat of Lucille's clapping and let herself be guided by Pearl's hands, and soon she was having so much fun she had to laugh out loud. Pearl laughed, too, and when the song ended, they both bent over, holding their sides and panting. Neither of them noticed Sadie come down the steps.

"Those are your two fine girls," Lucille said happily. "Ain't you proud of them, Sadie?"

Eva and Pearl both straightened up quickly, still giggling.

Sadie stood on the bottom step and looked over the scene. "Proud that they've got to dance in a whorehouse?" she asked. "No, Lucille, I ain't proud."

There was a moment of tense, painful silence until Sadie walked back up the steps, the other women rose from the overstuffed chairs as if they had someplace to go, and Eva's dance lesson was over.

Maybe it was to try to lift everyone's mood after Sadie's "accident" with the laudanum, but Miss B decided a little bit of alcohol wouldn't do the girls any harm. So after supper she served a couple rounds of beer in the parlor, with lemonade for Eva and Pearl. At first everyone laughed and joked. But on the second round, Ida starting in telling about her childhood on a homestead in Kansas. "It was the winter I turned nine," Ida said mournfully. "First Mama, then Papa, dead from the influenza."

Pearl rolled her eyes and nudged Eva. "Here we go again. All it takes is two beers, and out come the sad stories."

"Not one—not a single one—of my no-good relatives would take me in," Ida said. "They shipped me off to that damn orphanage in Topeka. I'm telling you, the caretakers there would rather beat a child than feed her." She recounted how, by the age of thirteen, she was an experienced thief, and she'd had enough of the harsh treatment in the orphanage. "I figured that old witch of a director could afford a few dollars to buy me a ticket out of there, so I stole her money purse and got on a train to Denver. Met a recruiter on my first day in town, and I haven't been hungry a day since," she said. Then she added, a little too loudly, "Ain't that right, Miss B?"

Miss B smiled as she poured a bit more beer into Ida's mug, then held up her hand to signify that was all she was getting.

Ruby's was the next story to come out. "I grew up back east in Virginia. My mother and father, they were nice folks, and I've got lots of brothers and sisters—I reckon they're mostly grown by now. I was already eighteen with no beau, and one day I read in the newspaper about men in the west needing wives. So I wrote a letter the way the newspaper said to do. I got an answer from a miner—George Durbin, his name was. He seemed nice enough. He wrote me sweet-talking letters for months. Then he proposed marriage, bought me a train ticket to Colorado, and married me." She looked up at a place on the ceiling as if she could see the past up there. She took a long swig of beer. "One day he walked out and never came back. Left me a note that said don't wait for him. Even if I'd *had* the money for cross-country train fare, I couldn't have gone back to Virginia in disgrace with my husband disappeared. I had to figure out a way to take care of myself." Her eyes shifted nervously in Miss B's direction. "Miss B helped me get on my feet." She hesitated. "And I'm *glad* of it."

Then Lucille started in. "I never minded farmwork. Back in Iowa we had a hundred and sixty acres. I liked my mama and daddy and my brothers just fine. But I had one uncle—he liked me *too* much, you might say. When I told my mama, she didn't believe me, and when I told my daddy, he smacked me across the face so hard it knocked me down. When a recruiter came to our town, I figured I might as well get paid to do what I already had to do for free, so I came to Denver."

When there was silence and it seemed to be Sadie's turn to reminisce, Eva watched her expectantly. Sadie sighed. "My baby sister, Rose, is seventeen now. Ma and Pa lived just long enough to see her grown and married off."

Eva slumped a little. So her grandparents were dead. She wondered if Pearl had been able to visit them. But she had an aunt! Aunt Rose. Now she had two aunts she'd never met: Aunt Linnie in South Carolina and Aunt Rose in . . . where?

"Where?" she said out loud, surprising even herself.

"What?" Sadie asked.

"Where does Rose live?" Eva asked.

"Oh, she lives in Nebraska, but there's no point worrying about that," Pearl chimed in. "You think anybody here gets a visit from their family *or* can go back home? Quickest way to get disowned, as far as I can see, is move to Holladay Street—and that's no matter how much money they send home at Christmastime," she said bitterly.

Miss B, hearing that the conversation was headed downhill, announced that it was high time for everyone to get ready for work.

"Come on, Eva," said Pearl. "I got to show you how to get dressed."

The blue dress and short, silky petticoat had hung in the wardrobe for a couple of days now, and the blue shoes had sat unused except for the one dance lesson. But Miss B was officially reopening the dance hall tonight, and Eva was its newest "attraction." She'd been looking forward to this night with a mixture of dread and excitement, and now it was here.

Upstairs in their bedroom, Pearl spoke with authority. "Always put your dress on before your powder," she commanded, and helped Eva pull the blue silk dress over her head. It fit perfectly and felt smooth against her skin. Her knees felt cold under the short hemline.

Pearl sat her down at the dressing table. "Remember, powder, but no rouge," she said.

Eva nodded. She closed her eyes, and Pearl smoothed the soft powder puff over her cheeks, nose, forehead, and chin. She opened her eyes to see Pearl grimacing at her.

"What's wrong?" Eva asked.

"You look dead," Pearl said. She looked from the powder jar to Eva. "The color's all wrong. You got to tell Miss B to get you some of that powder they make for colored girls. They got all shades, even light like you."

Eva glanced in the mirror and hoped she wouldn't look that bad when she *was* dead. She washed in the basin, scrubbing the pink powder away.

Miss B had given Eva new silver hair combs. Pearl supervised as Eva redid her braid, then tucked the silver combs into the sides of her hair. "Here, you can borrow this, too," Pearl said, and fastened a chain with a silver locket around Eva's neck.

Eva touched the locket. "Thank you," she said. Already the girl in the mirror looked less like her and more like a sophisticated showgirl.

"Now pinch your cheeks like this." Pearl demonstrated, grinning conspiratorially. "It makes us *look* like we're wearing rouge!"

While Eva slowly and carefully pulled on her black silk stockings—Pearl had warned her not to run them—Pearl got herself ready.

"Lord, Eva, you're slow. I'm going out to use the privy—my customers waited so many days to dance with me, I reckon there won't be time for me to go out back again until midnight."

Eva fastened her garters, slipped her feet into the soft blue shoes, and took one last look in the mirror. The royal blue dress seemed to glow in the light of the kerosene lamp, and the silver locket and hair combs glittered. The girl in the mirror looked a little scared but more beautiful than Eva had ever imagined she could be. She took a deep breath, then let it out, willing herself to be calm. Dancing with Pearl had been fun, she reminded herself. And she would be making money—piles of it. "This is it, Mama Kate," she whispered. "Wish me luck." She straightened herself up and headed downstairs to the dance hall.

Eva heard "Wait for the Wagon" being pounded out on the piano well before she entered the crowded room. Smoke filled the air and curled upward from cigars and pipes. Obviously Miss B's rules about "no colored" only pertained to what went on in the upstairs rooms. Leaning against the bar, standing in groups, or playing cards at the tables were black men, white men, Spanish men. She saw no Indians or Chinese, which didn't surprise her. There were lots of places where Indians and Chinese were not welcome. A round-faced black man in a neatly tailored shirt and fine gray breeches sat at the piano, his hands dancing over the keys. That must be "The Professor," as the girls called him, Eva thought.

"Eva!" Ruby called to her from across the crowd, and motioned her over.

Eva pushed her way past rawhide vests and scruffy beards, and *everyone,* it seemed, turned to stare at her as she passed.

"Here's a boy wants to dance with you!" Ruby still had to shout to be heard over the music and loud voices.

Eva's stomach lurched. *Already?* But when she saw the boy, she calmed a bit. He was not much taller than she, almost too young to shave, holding his hat in his hands and looking terrified as a group of men pushed him forward, teasing and laughing.

"Come on, Carlos, dance with her," they called. "Yeah, Carlos, get the first dance. You know the first is always the best!" The men all erupted in wild laughter, and Carlos grinned shyly.

Ruby nudged Eva. "This isn't a public dance, honey. Make him pay the bartender."

Carlos heard, fished a twenty-five-cent piece out of his boot, and placed it on the bar. The bartender, Gus, a beefy white man with more hair on his face than on his head, snatched it up and nodded at Eva.

Ruby gave Eva a little shove. "Go on, honey. The secret to this business is turnover. The quicker you start and get it over with, the sooner you can get another paying customer."

The Professor had begun to play "Beautiful Dreamer," and Ruby leaned on the piano to sing, "Beautiful dreamer, wake unto me, starlight and dewdrops are waiting for thee. . . ."

Eva wished Carlos would put down his hat and take her hand, show *her* what to do. But it was clear that she would have to take charge. With a surge of determination she grabbed his hat, threw it onto the back of a chair, and yanked him onto the dance floor.

Once there, Carlos surprised her. With one hand lightly on her waist and the other holding hers, he led her gracefully in the steps and turns of the waltz. Ruby's clear, high voice rang out, "Sounds of the rude world heard in the day, lulled by the moonlight have all passed away. . . ." Eva rested one hand on Carlos's shoulder but never had to push to keep him from pulling her too close—a trick Pearl had taught her. He was too shy to even look at her, and when the dance was over, he scurried back to get his hat amid the cheers and applause of his friends. Eva sighed. There was no hope of him buying her one of those expensive cocktails. But it had been a lovely dance, and she felt elated at her success.

She turned to find Ruby but saw that she was already leaving on the arm of a burly man in a long black frock coat. Pearl had explained how Sadie and the others only came to the dance hall when they didn't already have a customer waiting for them in the parlor and that they tried to rustle one up as soon as possible. Only she and Pearl would dance all evening.

The dance, combined with her nervousness, had made her thirsty. She leaned over the bar. "Gus, can I have a glass of water?" she called over the loud piano.

"That'll be one dollar," Gus said as he lifted a glass down off the shelf. "I'll take it out of your pay."

Eva stared at him, hoping to see a sign that he was joking. He wasn't.

"Poor thing. She hasn't gotten anybody to buy her a drink yet," Gus said mockingly. Then he scowled and pointed one finger at her. "You're supposed to be out there hawking drinks, wench."

The insult hit her like a punch in the stomach. She turned away, trying to focus on the crowd, hoping that Carlos might find her for another dance and this time buy her a cocktail. Someone took her arm roughly.

"Here you go, Gus," the man said as he threw coins onto the bar. "I'm buying her for two."

Eva found herself being dragged onto the dance floor by a short, wide man with an unkempt beard and teeth so stained with tobacco that when he grinned, it looked as if his mouth was full of worms.

"You're the prettiest girl they ever brought in here," he said. He pulled her close and breathed rank tobacco and whiskey breath over her. "When you gonna start working upstairs?"

"I'm not!" Eva struggled to get her hand onto his shoulder so she could push him away, but he just tightened his grip as she squirmed. She tried to stomp his feet, but her soft dancing slippers could hardly be felt through his thick boots.

"You're missing the steps, there, sweetheart." He laughed into her face, and she nearly gagged on his breath. "Here, let me help you out."

He pressed his body firmly into hers and wheeled her around the dance floor. She felt helpless, disgusted. Her relief when the song ended was short-lived. He'd paid for two! When he finally let her go, she was limp from the struggle, wet from his perspiration and hers, sure she smelled of his stench, and nauseated from the whole ordeal.

"Now, if you'd a been nice, I'd invite you for a drink. But you been downright difficult," he said, and walked off.

Eva choked on tears. Pearl whirled by and leaned toward

her. "I forgot to teach you the hat pin trick," she called over the music. "But sometimes it doesn't work anyway." She shrugged and danced off. Pearl's partner was holding her closer than Eva ever wanted to be held again.

She felt dizzy and very thirsty. She'd only brought in seventy-five cents, and by the time the bartender and Miss B got their cuts, that would be down to pennies. But if she had to endure another dance like the one she'd just been through, she would surely vomit onto the dance floor. Her head throbbed. Maybe Gerta was in the kitchen and would fix her some warm milk and nutmeg. She headed toward the door.

"You can't leave!" It was Pearl, catching up to her. "The night just started."

"I"—Eva held her aching head—"I can't do this."

Pearl stomped one foot and grunted with disgust. "Shoot, Eva, it's just dancing. Would you rather work upstairs?"

"No!" Eva shouted it.

"Here." Pearl pulled a long, wicked-looking hat pin out of her hair. "Hide this in your hair and *use* it. Sometimes it helps."

"Sometimes?" Eva asked weakly.

Pearl crossed her arms over her chest. "If you don't dance, how are you going to pay for that dress? And the shoes and silk stockings, and all the food you ate this week, and the silver hair combs—how are you going to pay?" she demanded. Her tone was angry, but Eva saw fear in Pearl's eyes.

Eva squared her shoulders. "I'll take in laundry," she announced, and was suddenly relieved. Of course. Why hadn't she decided to do that in the first place?

Pearl let out one harsh laugh. "And pay for that hundred-dollar dress? You'll be ninety years old before you pay it off." A tall man with legs lanky as a colt's tapped Pearl's arm. She turned, smiled coyly, and let him lead her to the dance floor.

A hundred-dollar dress? Eva reeled. This dress was worth more money than the house she'd grown up in. And *she* had to pay for it? Pay for everything else, too? She felt like throwing the silver hair combs in Miss B's face. She'd thought they were a gift! Suddenly fifty cents for each cocktail seemed like nothing. She would be in debt to Miss B forever.

A man with wet liver lips and deep set dark eyes peered at her. "Gus says you're the new girl, and I just paid for a dance and a cocktail, so let's go."

Eva reluctantly took his hand. During the dance she held her breath against his body odor and whiskey breath and tried to think only of the glass of cool colored water that awaited her. When the dance was over and she sat drinking her "cocktail," she pasted on a smile and nodded as if she was listening to her host yammering about the lode of gold he was sure to find up in the mines near Central City. As the evening wore on, she felt farther and farther from her body, as if she was watching some other young girl be grabbed and held close and swung around the dance floor by sweaty, unwashed miners and cowhands. She used the hat pin a few times, stabbing it into a man's hand or arm when he got fresh. Sometimes it worked, but sometimes the man just called her "feisty" or "hot tamale" and snuggled in closer. She went from dance floor to bar stool and back again in a daze until midnight came and the Professor told Eva and Pearl they were free to go.

Eva stepped out back to use the privy, and when the brisk night air brushed her face, it seemed to slam her mind back into her body. She smelled the smoke and men's sweat on her dress, felt the bruises on her hips where she'd been pressed into belt buckles, remembered the groping and the rank breath in her face. There, under a sky filled with brilliant stars, she fell to her knees on the ground and vomited.

In the morning, Eva's new silk dress was gone and her Sunday dress hung over the chair, freshly laundered. Martha must have come in while she was sleeping, she thought. She wished the silk dress was gone for good but knew it was only being cleaned because of the mess she'd made of it when she'd gotten sick out back. Ruby, in between customers, had found her, helped her clean up, and tucked her into bed. The last thing Ruby had said was, "You'll get used to it, honey. We all did."

Eva pulled the covers up over her face to blot out the sunlight. She hoped Mama Kate was listening to her thoughts. *It's not what I thought it would be, Mama Kate, really it's not. I thought it would be fun to dress up the way Pearl does, and it was, until* . . . Remembering made her queasy, so she tried not to think about last night. *And now I owe Miss B so much money. . . .* She sniffled loudly. Pearl shoved her.

"You under there sniffling and crying like a baby?" Pearl yanked the covers down. "I got no patience with your sulking. You're acting like somebody made you sell your soul to the devil." Pearl sat up in bed. "You got a better idea what to do with yourself?" When Eva didn't answer, she propped her pillows up against the bedstead and leaned back. "Here's how I see it. Being a girl, you got three ways to go." She counted them on her fingers. "You can sell yourself as a shopgirl—work all your waking hours, ruin your feet, and still not have enough to eat." Next finger. "You can sell yourself in marriage to some clod-hopper husband, and if you're *lucky,* you eat and don't get beat." Last finger. "Or you can sell yourself in a place like this, where the eating is darn good." As if to emphasize her point, the smell of baking sweet cakes for breakfast wafted up the steps.

Eva wiped her nose with the back of her hand. "I wish I'd thought to start taking in laundry before Miss B bought me all these fancy clothes."

Pearl looked at her cross-eyed. "You *are* a hayseed, ain't you? Nobody but Chinese does laundry here in Denver. It's almost like a law or something. Even the colored women complain about it."

Eva sighed heavily. "But why not a shopgirl?" She'd seen the skinny, mousy girls behind the counters in the shops, and that job now seemed like an excellent one compared to dancing.

Pearl snorted. "Because it doesn't *work*—unless your daddy owns the shop," she said harshly. "Mama tried it, you know that? When she first came to Denver. She wanted a job where she could feed herself and send money back home. But the men who own those shops pay the girls hardly two cents to keep them from starving. She was renting a room with no heat, sleeping in all her clothes, and when her one dress started looking shabby, the shopkeeper told her not to come back until she made a new one. Well, she didn't have no extra money for calico or thread or a needle. So that was that." Pearl brushed her hands together as if she was ridding them of flour.

Eva was horrified by the thought of it: Sadie, coming to Denver from her family farm in Nebraska, hardly older than Pearl and just as much an innocent country girl as Eva herself. As awful as the dancing was, what must it have been like for Sadie, in desperation, to take a job working upstairs in a brothel?

"It's not fair," Eva said in a small voice.

"Is that all you can think about? What's fair and what's not fair?" Pearl tossed the covers off and swung her legs over the side of the bed. "I done earned my breakfast—I'm going to go eat."

Eva washed the tears from her face, combed her hair and braided it, and put on her gingham dress. At least she could dress like herself during the day, wear her long cotton petticoat with the silver dollar in it that reminded her of Mama Kate and home. And she could try not to think about what the evening would bring.

At breakfast they passed around a platter of fried egg sandwiches with sliced raw onions and a dish of cinnamon cakes.

"Eva, you did a fine job dancing last night," said Ruby, trying to sound encouraging.

"Except she retched all over herself afterward," said Pearl.

Ruby shot Pearl a nasty look, and Eva felt her face heat up with embarrassment.

Miss B came in and slapped a copy of the *Denver Times* down on the table. "The newspaper says there's a senator in town with his wife and children," she announced. "They're on their way into the mountains for the camp cure." She smiled slyly. "Anyone for betting which house he spends his evenings at while they're in town?"

"I wager two dollars he goes to Belle Birnard's," said Lucille. "That's where all the politicians go."

"I'm betting on Mattie Silks," said Ruby. "That new house of hers is the highest class—all crystal chandeliers, cigars from Havana, and fine Rhine wines." She waved her hands as if she were pointing out these luxuries.

"And how come you know so much about the high-class houses?" Ida leaned toward Ruby in a playful challenge. "Is that where you been working on your day off?"

There was laughter around the table. Miss B bet her money on Mattie Silks as well, saying that her house, which was just down the street, never looked so fancy before Mattie moved in with her girls.

Each day, as evening approached, Eva felt herself stepping aside from her body, closing her mind to what awaited her on the dance floor. Each night she went through the motions of dancing, smiling, saying thank you for the sugary cocktails as if she was watching it all from someplace else, holding her breath, waiting for the moment when she could exhale and be herself again. The moment of exhale usually came as she lay in the darkness of her bedroom, her silk dress in a heap on the floor, trying to remember a day with Mama Kate and Daddy Walter—a day of good hard work like gardening or scrubbing the floors, with smells of rich earth and lye soap instead of cigars and whiskey and strange men. She'd listen to Pearl's rhythmic breathing beside her in bed and wonder how she had stood this life all these years. Did Pearl, as a four-year-old, question why she wasn't allowed in her mother's bedroom at night when she woke with a bad dream? Did Pearl, as a seven-year-old, know what her mother did for work? Did she ever ask who her father was, or did she simply figure there was no way for Sadie to know for sure?

Eva wondered if she'd ever get used to this life the way Pearl had. She talked to Mama Kate less and less. Certainly Mama Kate knew what she was doing, and Eva was sure she didn't approve, and so there was nothing to say. It was no use defending herself: she *should* have known not to order the dress and other fineries. She should have been stronger, prouder. But now, nightly, she was pushed and prodded and made to go exactly where she did not want to go, and she knew without a doubt that she was not making Mama Kate glad.

Another Sunday came and went and Eva didn't go to visit Mr. Stonewall and attend church. There was too much to hide from him now, and she was too ashamed of it all.

Yet within Miss B's house, no one thought she had anything to be ashamed of. Pearl offered advice on how to fend off the "mashers," but other than that no one even mentioned the ordeal Eva faced each night. Sadie, in particular, made sure Eva knew she was *lucky* to be where she was. Out of the blue she would come up with statements like, "Ida says at that orphanage where she got sent, they beat the girls with a leather strap. If you don't believe her, take a look at the backs of her legs next time she's in the bath." After a moment's thought, Eva would understand that Sadie was saying, "Just be glad you're not in an orphanage."

Another time she said, "Back home we were all so poor, my cousin Camilla got married off when she was thirteen. Her daddy didn't want to feed her anymore. Could you imagine? At *thirteen* having to start taking care of a man and having babies and what all."

And another time: "Mary Gallagan got arrested last night. Turns out she had two underage girls working in her house *upstairs,* one thirteen and one only eleven years old."

And another: "Gerta, I think your cooking agrees with Eva. She don't look so skinny like she did when she first got here."

This last statement made Eva angry because, though it was

true that she'd been hungry at times living on the homestead, she didn't think it was Sadie's place to mention it. Maybe the anger was a good thing: it pushed Eva to corner Sadie one night after midnight as Eva trudged up the stairs to bed and Sadie happened to be in the hallway.

"I like the food here, but Mama Kate and Daddy Walter fed me just fine." Eva said it bluntly, angrily.

Sadie looked weary. She leaned one shoulder against the wall. "I'm sure they did," she said.

A golden moment. Sadie alone. Eva's mind rushed to her unanswered questions. "What was my father's name?" she blurted out.

Sadie closed her eyes, thinking. "Joseph," she said. "Yes, that was it."

"Joseph," Eva repeated. A real person. She wanted Sadie to tell her *everything* she knew about him, every last detail. "Tell me—" she began.

"He was a miner. That's all I know. Never told me a blasted thing about where he was from or his ma or pa, which is what I'm sure you want to know. That's not the kind of thing you talk about when you're doing business. He was skinny and tall." She shrugged. "That's all I can tell you."

Eva looked down at the flowered carpet. She was about to say thank you, about to pick another of her burning questions and blurt it out, about to ask, "Did you miss me when you gave me away?" when a horrifying scream rang out.

Sadie whipped around. "Ruby!" she cried.

Everything started happening at once: Sadie bashing into Ruby's room, Miss B running up the steps two at a time, Ida and Lucille rushing down the hall, silk dressing gowns flying. Ida grabbed Eva's arm. "We got to help," she cried, and pulled Eva into Ruby's room.

A heavy man, dressed only in underdrawers, knelt over Ruby. He was shaking her by the throat, banging her head against the floor. Ruby's eyes were closed, her mouth now open and silent. Sadie grabbed the fire poker and swung, and Eva heard a sickening crack as it connected with the back of the man's head. He fell sideways, a limp pile of white flesh.

"She's breathing," Lucille said, holding Ruby's head.

But when they lifted Ruby onto the bed, jostled her, and even shouted at her, she did not respond.

"I'll fetch the smelling salts," said Miss B. "*And* the police."

Sadie stood over the man, ready with the fire poker. On her way out, Miss B handed Sadie her revolver. "If he comes to, shove this in his face. That ought to make him behave."

Eva blinked at Sadie as she stood with the gun in both hands. She was stunned by Sadie's strength and resolve. She hadn't been afraid to swing the poker, and Eva had no doubt that she wouldn't be afraid to fire the revolver if she had to.

Ida wet a handkerchief in the washbasin, and when she applied the cold cloth to Ruby's neck, Ruby's eyes fluttered open.

"There she is!" Lucille laughed with relief.

"Lord, my throat," Ruby moaned. "And my *head.*"

Eva drenched a second cloth and applied it to Ruby's forehead.

"He just go crazy on you?" Lucille asked.

Ruby nodded, then held her head because nodding hurt. "He was calling me by some other name—Jackie, I think it was—and getting real mean and vile. He's so liquored up if you put a match to him, he'll light like a torch."

The man stirred slightly, and Sadie straightened her arms, aiming the pistol squarely at his face. Miss B came huffing up the steps, followed by a uniformed police officer.

How convenient, Eva thought, *he must have just been stopping by.* Miss B and Sadie helped the officer drag the still-unconscious man down the back staircase that led to the kitchen. Eva knew without anyone telling her that everything would be done to protect the man, to make sure that his wife, family, and business associates never found out that he had attacked a woman in a brothel. Eva also knew that no one would ask Ruby if she wanted to press charges. For her, it was considered part of her job.

Ruby fell asleep, and Lucille climbed into bed with her so she wouldn't be alone. Ida freshened the cloth on Ruby's forehead. "That got rid of my all-night guest in a hurry," Ida said.

"He run off as soon as he heard the commotion. Good thing he paid up front." She shuffled off to her room.

Eva walked slowly to her own bedroom. Her hands shook as she lit the kerosene lamp. Pearl came in, looking worried. "Is Ruby going to be all right?" she asked.

"Where were *you*?" Eva snapped, as if Pearl's absence had caused the whole thing.

"Miss B made me stay and be charming with the men waiting in the parlor so they wouldn't get suspicious," Pearl said defensively.

"Oh," Eva said. "Ruby's all right, just her head hurts and her neck hurts and she's shook up."

Pearl grimaced. "Poor Ruby," she said.

Lying in bed, Eva wished she could talk to Mama Kate about it, tell her what a horrible thing had just happened and how much it scared her. But Mama Kate seemed far away now, as if she had gotten plain disgusted with what she saw Eva doing each night, had given up on watching over her, and had left her really, truly on her own.

The senator, it turned out, spent three evenings in a row at Mattie Silks's sporting house before taking his family up into the mountains for the camp cure. The newspapers reported that he'd left town and that the camp cure—spending several weeks in the rarefied air of the mountains with horse and carriage, tents, cots, and a cook—had been prescribed for his youngest son's breathing difficulties. The newspapers, of course, did not report the senator's visits to Mattie Silks's establishment any more than they reported it when judges, rich lawyers, bankers, doctors, and politicians of every level spent their free time and extra cash in the fanciest houses on Holladay Street.

"That Mattie Silks, she's going to make her mark on this town," said Miss B, one evening at the supper table. "I heard she bought forty thousand dollars' worth of furniture, fine art, crystal chandeliers, and Oriental rugs just to get started!"

But Lucille quickly assured her. "I ain't jealous of no Miss Mattie—or her girls." Lucille said she was happy at Miss B's house with "down-home" folks like policemen, carpenters, shop owners, and the occasional miner who'd struck a lode and had extra cash. "They got better morals than those uppity rich fellas," said Lucille. "They don't expect craziness when they take you upstairs." The other girls agreed: they were happy that their customers were the good, solid, hardworking clientele at Miss B's. Nobody mentioned the man who'd almost killed Ruby.

Ruby's throat showed two purple bruises where the "guest" had dug in his thumbs. Ruby took a few days of rest to let herself heal a bit, then tied a scarf around her neck and went back to work. She never complained about what had happened. Eva had the uneasy feeling that it was not the first time these women had fought off a violent customer. Why else would they have been so organized, as if they'd practiced for the battle? She was quietly relieved to know that Sadie was a terror with that fire poker.

One morning Miss B showed Eva her books—or the page in her books that held Eva's account. There was the cost of the dress added to the price of the combs, shoes, and stockings, along with ten days of "room and board," which Eva understood represented her bed and meals.

"How much money do you have?" Miss B demanded.

"None." Eva began to explain that Gus hadn't given her any money, that all of her dance and cocktail money had gone to him. Then she remembered the few coins Mr. Harper had given her and Mama Kate's silver dollar. "A little," she said in a small voice.

"Bring it to me," Miss B ordered.

Eva walked slowly up the steps. *Don't use this unless there's* nothing *else you can do.* Mama Kate's words. *Well, Mama Kate, what I can do is not tell her about it.*

In her bedroom Eva reached into the bottom of her carpet-bag and pulled out the coins Mr. Harper had given to her: three dimes. She went downstairs and handed them over to Miss B.

Miss B recorded the dimes in her book, along with the money Eva had earned from dances and cocktails and one "tip" of fifty cents, which had come from some unidentified admirer. Eva studied the numbers for a moment. She still owed so much more than she'd earned. But at least she had paid back *some-thing.* Would she be able to pay back her whole debt within a couple of years if she worked very hard at dancing and flirting? The thought sickened her as she saw, stretched before her, years of dancing every night with stinking, gruff men who mashed her to their bodies with no concern for her feelings. She bit her lip and nodded to Miss B that she understood. Miss B handed her one dime. "Spend this as you like," she said.

Eva held the dime, just looking at it, thinking there was nothing she wanted to buy so much as her way out of this house. She was about to hand it back to Miss B and tell her to use it toward her debt when Pearl ducked her head in.

"Miss B pay you that dime yet?" Pearl asked. "She said you'd take us for ice cream."

"Go on, girls." Miss B shooed them out of her study. "Get your ice cream and be back for supper."

Eva saw that she had no choice in the matter. Pearl ran up the steps to get her shawl, and Eva followed her. "Since when do I have to take *you* for ice cream?" she demanded.

"Since Miss B paid you a whole dime—that'll buy us each one."

"Didn't Miss B pay *you*?" Pearl didn't even have new clothes to pay off. How dare she spend Eva's hard-earned money?

Pearl shook her head. "I told her to put my pay toward Mama's doctor costs."

Eva froze inside. Sadie was in debt, too? And with the kind of cash she brought in working upstairs? Eva had seen the money exchange hands—a ten-dollar gold piece from a guest to Miss B to buy a brass token. Each morning, Sadie, Ida, Ruby, and Lucille dropped their handfuls of tokens onto Miss B's desk for her to record their earnings. They got half of what was taken in. Eva had examined one of the tokens once. It was the size of a silver dollar, with words pressed into it like on a coin: DENVER, COLO., MADAM BLANCHE BEAUMONT, PROPRIETOR, GOOD FOR ONE SCREW. About five or six guests came and went from each girl's room in a night. Eva would never have dreamed that Sadie could owe anyone money.

Pearl saw the perplexed look on Eva's face. "All those years when I was little and could eat but couldn't work yet, and always getting the croup, and Doc Stevens being called so often his wife started to worry he had other business here." Pearl smiled a little. "Mama got down on her cash." She looked more serious. "And Doc Stevens being called last week didn't help none. Miss B is carrying it for her, and the past few years I been helping her pay it off."

Eva felt shaken. *Lord,* she thought, *so if you get sick in this place, or wear out your silk dress and need a new one, or Miss B gives you a piece of jewelry that looks like a gift. . . .* The debt was like prison chains holding Sadie here. And what of the others? Did they owe money on dresses and doctor bills? Ida said she'd had two pregnancies the doctor had to "take care of." And Lucille said she'd been "clapped up" once, despite all the precautions they took at Miss B's, and needed medicine to cure her. Though they'd each come willingly to this house, were they all now held here, unable to break away even if they wanted to? Of course, Eva thought, why else would Ruby stay even after she'd been nearly murdered? Mama Kate's words came back to her: *You're the first one in this family born free. Wherever you go, you be proud and strong so it's clear that you know in your bones that you're free.*

"Oh no!" Eva said out loud.

"What?" Pearl asked.

But Eva just shook her head. *I've lost it all,* she thought, *lost the freedom I had, shamed Mama Kate and Daddy Walter. . . .*

Pearl grew impatient. "You want to go for ice cream or not?" she demanded.

What did it matter now? She needed something to cheer her up. "I'll go," Eva said.

Dressed in their gingham and wrapped in their shawls against a crisp, cold wind, the girls cut across 19th to Larimer Street, toward the Standley Fruit and Confectionery Shop, which Pearl said was the best in town. This time Pearl walked beside Eva instead of marching on ahead. The wooden sidewalk was wet—a rain shower had just swept through—and huge gray thunderclouds still billowed and moved across the blue sky. The mountains were shimmering white giants, covered with new snowfall.

They passed Mrs. Camelleri's restaurant with the line for an early supper already snaking into the street. The men who stood outside whistled at the girls and shouted to them. A few called out, "Save me a dance tonight, sweetheart!" Pearl answered, "Just bring your cash, boys." Eva kept her eyes on the sidewalk and walked briskly. But she couldn't help glancing up once, and there she saw Carlos standing quietly in line. He watched her but didn't call out. When she met his eyes, he smiled slightly and looked away. *For you,* she thought, *I would save a dance.* In fact, she wished he'd strike a lode of gold and come pay for all of her dances every night, whirling her around the dance floor in that polite, shy way of his and saving her from all the lecherous older men. But she hadn't seen him since that first night, so she guessed he needed to spend all his money on food, not dancing.

She dared not smile back—she didn't want any of the other men to think she was smiling at them—so she looked down and hurried by.

Before they reached the confectionery, Pearl stopped and touched Eva's shoulder. "I dare you to walk past the cribs," she whispered.

Eva didn't know what the "cribs" were, but she could tell from Pearl's expression that they were something sordid. She wasn't about to back down from a dare. "I dare you to come with me," she shot back.

Pearl nodded conspiratorially. "The girls are probably still asleep," she said. "But we'll walk real fast and just take a peek. If there's a girl in a doorway, don't look at her, and if she touches you, *scream* and run like hell."

Eva felt perspiration break out on her back. What in the world was she getting herself into?

Pearl led her up Larimer to 22nd Street and then back across to Holladay Street. To Eva, it seemed as if they had entered another world. Here, only blocks away from their own lovely section of Holladay, the houses were one-story wooden structures, shacks, really, built attached in a row, each with an ill-fitting door and one window. The muddy roadway was strewn with garbage, and a rat scuttled by in front of them. There was a horrible stench—Eva guessed it was coming from the dead tabby cat lying in the road with its belly skyward. An old black man walked by using a cane and gave them the evil eye as if trying to turn them back. Eva's stomach churned. She *wanted* to turn back.

"Pearl," Eva began, ready to give up on the dare.

But Pearl was leaning into a window, her hands cupped around her eyes. She motioned Eva to shush, then waved her to come see. The window was greasy with soot, adorned on the inside with a stained yellow curtain. The curtain had a hole cut in it, right at eye level, as if inviting passersby to peek in.

"This is how they advertise," Pearl said, pointing to the peephole. She snickered with contempt. "Hurry up!" She nudged Eva toward the window.

Eva cupped her hands and looked in. The tiny room held a trunk, a washstand, and a plain narrow bed. A ratty-looking quilt lay crumpled on the floor, and the sheet covering the bed was gray with use and age. The stench of the dead cat wafted to her on the wind. Eva turned away, nauseated.

"She probably just got up. I bet she's out back using the privy," said Pearl. "We'd better get out of here before—"

The door to a room nearby flew open. A woman charged out. She was large and wild-eyed, with long gray hair tumbling down her back. Her wrinkled cheeks were caked with rouge and powder. She shrieked, lunged at Pearl, clamped a clawlike hand into Pearl's hair. Pearl screamed and kicked the woman's leg so hard she let go and doubled over.

"Run!" Pearl shouted.

The two girls ran past the shacks, with their doors flying open and disheveled-looking women peering out, past the dead cat, past the old man with the cane, and back around the corner to Larimer Street.

There they stopped, chests heaving, sweating in the cold wind. Eva wanted to weep. "Who *are* they?" she gasped. "Why do they live like that?"

Pearl stared at her crossly, as if Eva was an idiot not to understand what she had just seen. Then she softened a bit. "They didn't teach you nothing on that homestead of yours or in that school you used to go to, did they?" she said.

Eva didn't know how to answer. Pearl reached out and brushed back a strand of Eva's hair that had gotten stuck in the sweat on her cheek. "All you need to know is we ain't ever going to end up there—not you or me or Mama, not Lucille or the other girls either. Not ever. Mama says she'll find a good man for a husband before she gets too old to work for Miss B." Pearl wiped the sweat from her own face with her shawl. "Come on, let's get our ice cream."

It was only the second time in her life Eva had tasted ice cream. It should have been a wonderful experience, like it had been the first time, under the tent at the country fair. Mama Kate and Daddy Walter had laughed as they watched her eyes pop open wide at the cold sweetness of it. But this time it tasted heavy and sat like a rock in her stomach. Maybe it was the smell of that dead cat that she couldn't quite get out of her nostrils. Or maybe it was the faces of those women in their wretched doorways. All their powder and rouge couldn't cover their despair.

The bitterness of what she'd seen settled on Eva's tongue like a dose of quinine. What she didn't know then was that it was only the beginning of what would be a very, very bitter night.

Eva and Pearl entered the house to the sounds of an argument raging upstairs—Sadie and Miss B.

"No! I won't allow it!" It was Sadie, more defiant of her madam than Eva had ever known her to be.

"Then you'll not have your room here either. I'll have you jailed for failure to pay your debt."

"You can't do it!" Now Sadie sounded close to tears. "Neither of them is even fifteen yet."

"For an extra handout, the city officials and police will believe they're whatever age I say they are—especially with no birth records to prove otherwise," Miss B said harshly. "I can't keep carrying this debt of yours. With your latest doctor bill it's higher than ever. You need help paying it off."

Pearl and Eva froze in the foyer. They stared at each other. The next thing they heard was the slamming of a door, then Sadie's ragged sobbing.

Miss B walked into the foyer. Eva and Pearl watched her in paralyzed silence. She gave them a disdainful look, then marched up the steps.

Pearl shook her head as if she was casting off a bad dream.

"Mama always said she'd get married and get us out of here before I got old enough to work upstairs. . . ."

"Sounds like she needs a marriage proposal right quick," said Eva.

Pearl scowled at her. "This ain't no time to joke. She's talking about *you*, too, you know."

Eva did know. But she also knew that Miss B had gone too far and that she, Eva, would be out of this house well before Miss B's plans came to pass. She had not totally forgotten Mama Kate's words about not getting pushed where she didn't want to go, about knowing in her bones that she was free. "She can talk all she wants," said Eva. "She just won't *get* what she wants because I won't be here."

"All you care about is yourself," Pearl snapped. "You run away, you know where Mama will end up? Jail. Debtors' prison because of *your* debt."

Eva narrowed her eyes at Pearl. "Are *you* going to stay and do what Miss B says?" she challenged.

"Hell, no," said Pearl. "I mean, I'll stay, but I won't do what she says." She crossed her arms over her chest. "I got hat pins, I got long fingernails, and I got teeth." She snapped her teeth together like an angry fox. "Ain't no client of Miss B's will want to be alone with *me* in an upstairs room."

But Ruby had told Eva stories about young girls being

drugged. . . . "Pearl, I don't think you should stay—" she began.

"I'll be *fine*," Pearl stopped her.

"I'll send back money for my debt," Eva offered.

Pearl threw up her hands. "How are you going to do that?"

"I don't know," Eva snapped. "But I've had enough of Miss B and her ideas."

Eva turned and stomped up the stairs. She was keenly aware of the silver dollar tapping against her leg as her petticoat swished with each step. A plan was forming in her mind. She would dance the evening through, then go upstairs to get her warm cape and boots and change into her gingham dress and long petticoat. She would leave the blue silk dress and dancing slippers forever. A trip out back to the privy would not end there but would take her all the way to Mr. Stonewall's house. He had told her to come to him if she needed help. Now she understood why he'd made that offer with such urgency.

Through supper and getting ready for the evening, Eva hardly spoke. Lucille asked her if she didn't feel well and placed a cool hand on Eva's forehead, but Eva just shook her head no.

Though she danced and smiled and nodded at the men who bought her cocktails, she didn't hear a word they said. She was thinking, hatching her plan. Her silver dollar would buy a train ticket, she hoped. Mr. Stonewall would know which train would take her to Georgetown, in the mountains. There she would find

Mrs. Santini. Poor as she was, surely Mrs. Santini would help her find work as a shopgirl or a governess or even a washwoman if the Chinese didn't do all the washing in Georgetown the way they did in Denver.

At the end of the evening, the Professor announced he would play one last waltz. Someone nudged Eva gently, and she turned to look, though her mind was still lost in scheming. At first she merely blinked at the person extending his hand to her for the dance. Just another male face, just another horrible dance. But when the person smiled shyly, Eva exclaimed, "Carlos!"

Carlos didn't say anything but swept her into the waltz, holding her neatly at arm's length and looking to the side to keep from bumping her into anything. Eva couldn't help but grin. *This* was the way dancing should feel, she thought, with the music nearly lifting her off the floor as she and Carlos flowed together, his hand lightly on her waist. She was even sorry when the dance ended.

Carlos didn't meet her eyes when he said thank you. He turned to go. But the same group of older men who had goaded him into asking her to dance that first night now shouted at him good-naturedly. "Invite her for a drink, Carlos!" "Come on, you cheapskate. Buy her a drink."

Carlos just shook his head until one of the men slapped a quarter down on the bar. "Pitch in, boys. He's afraid his mother will starve if he buys the girl a drink."

Several of his other friends produced quarters and a dime. Gus scooped up the coins and served a beer and a cocktail. Eva sat on one of the bar stools next to Carlos.

Carlos wasn't chattery like many of the men she'd met, but in response to her questions, he did tell her about himself. He spoke with a slight Spanish accent and told her how he'd come from the New Mexico Territory to work in the mines two years ago when he was twelve years old. These days he was working in a gold mine near Central City, and he helped bring the ore to the Argo Smelter in Denver once a week or so. Most months he'd been able to send money home to his mother and five younger brothers and sisters. His mother was Mexican, and his father, who was white, had run off and left her with no one to take care of her. That's why he couldn't afford to buy her a drink, he explained apologetically.

It was the first time Eva had actually listened to the man—or in this case, the boy—who bought her a drink. It was the first time she'd been interested.

"If I had the money, I'd come dance with you every night that I'm in Denver—except Sundays," he said all in a rush, then blushed brightly.

Eva felt herself blush as well. "I like the way you dance," she said. "I wish you didn't have to pay." And she thought, *If I weren't leaving, we could be friends.*

Carlos stood to go. "I'll save a quarter for when we come back to Denver. I will see you then?"

Eva felt a twinge of disappointment and guilt as she lied. "Yes. I'll see you then."

And she walked out of the dance hall for what she had decided would be her last time.

Stay calm. Do it just like you planned, Eva told herself. She went quietly upstairs to change her clothes.

But Martha met her in the hallway. "Miss B says to give me that dress so I can launder it before tomorrow evening," she said.

No problem, thought Eva. The sooner she got rid of the smoke-reeking thing, the better. She stepped out of the dress and handed it to Martha. She shivered in her chemise and short petticoat.

"The shoes and stockings, too. She says they need washing," said Martha.

Eva couldn't argue with that. The dainty slippers had had enough whiskey spilled on them to make a fancy dessert. And she wanted her sturdy button-up shoes and warm stockings for the walk to Mr. Stonewall's and the train ride, anyway.

When Martha had gone, Eva opened the door to her room. Pearl was already in bed. The room was lit only by moonlight. Quietly she went to the chair where she kept her gingham dress and long petticoat. She hastily stepped into the petticoat and fastened it over the shorter one she was already wearing. On a chilly night a girl couldn't wear too many petticoats. Then she reached for the dress and touched only the chair back. She crouched down and felt the floor. Had it fallen? She found nothing. She pulled open the wardrobe—Pearl must have hung it up with her things. She reached blindly into the wardrobe. Her fingers touched only empty hangers and the bare wardrobe walls. Eva gasped.

"They're gone," came Pearl's voice from the bed. "Shoes, too."

"Shoes, too?" Eva echoed, incredulous.

"She knows we heard," said Pearl. "She knows what we—what *you*—would want to do."

The hair rose on Eva's arms as goose bumps covered her body. "Our . . . nightgowns?" she asked. It was one of those clear nights when everything began to freeze the moment the sun set.

In answer, Pearl flopped the quilt down to reveal her own bare arms. She, like Eva, was dressed in only bloomers, a chemise, and petticoats. She pulled the quilt back up. "It's not so bad under the covers. And once she's sure we won't run, she'll probably give them back."

Eva thought of her old calico dress. How she wished it was still hidden under the mattress! She shook with cold and rage. "I *will* run," she said, defiant.

Pearl rolled over and pulled the covers up around her face. "Good luck," she said with more than a hint of sarcasm.

Eva stood for a moment, breathing hard. She couldn't stay—*wouldn't* stay. But she couldn't run through the streets of Denver half naked. And Pearl wasn't about to let her use the bed quilt as a cape.

She stepped out into the hallway. All of the bedroom doors were closed. It was early by "upstairs" standards, so the girls were most definitely still conducting business. The last thing Eva wanted to do was open one of the bedroom doors to grab a quilt.

She couldn't go down the front steps. Those led to the front parlor, which was filled with gentlemen guests drinking wine, smoking cigars, and chatting with Miss B while waiting for their turn upstairs. But there was the back stairwell: splintery, unfinished wooden steps that led directly to the kitchen. If she could enter the kitchen when neither Gerta nor Martha was there washing wineglasses or emptying ashtrays, then she could slip out the back door. And on her way out, she would grab a tablecloth to wrap around herself. *Mama Kate,* she said silently, *I'm leaving this place. I hope you'll help me however you can.*

The stairwell was only dimly lit—one small window provided a square of moonlight. The steps creaked as Eva settled one bare foot and then another on the rough wood. Below her the kitchen was quiet. Gerta and Martha must be serving drinks in the parlor. She'd better go *now.*

She ran down the steps and entered the brightly lit kitchen.

She could hear voices from the parlor. She eyed the table. There were too many dishes strewn over it, covering the tablecloth—no time to clear them. Where were the clean tablecloths kept? She put one hand on a cabinet, but at that moment the kitchen door swung open and Martha hurried in.

"Oh!" Martha cried in surprise.

Eva groaned. Her plan was ruined! The thought crossed her mind to plead with Martha, beg her not to betray her, but Martha had always been so loyal to Miss B. . . .

Martha stared at her a moment. Then she turned her back and began to wash dirty glasses, humming softly. The message was clear.

Eva glanced up at the heavy yellow curtains, grasped them with both hands, and yanked. They came down, rod and all. She wrapped a curtain around her shivering body and fled out the back door. Martha never even turned around.

Outside, the frozen ground stung her feet and stones dug into her soles. She ran through the back alley and out onto 19th Street. Music came from saloons and dance halls, and men stood in small knots, talking and smoking. To steer clear of them, Eva ran down the middle of the road.

"Hey!" a man shouted. "I said, *hey,* what you runnin' from, sweetheart?" His words were slurred. Eva ran faster. Her ankle twisted in a wagon wheel rut and she yelped.

The news of the spectacle seemed to travel down the street.

"Catch that woman—let *me* give her something to run from!" someone called out, and a whole group of men laughed.

Eva heard footsteps behind her. She tried to go faster, but pain shot through her ankle and she stumbled. Strong arms closed around her.

"I've got her," came a voice close to her ear.

Eva found herself looking into the pasty white face of a police officer. At first he appeared entertained, reveling in the sport of catching her. Then his face twisted.

"Ah, God, it's a child, not a woman. Who are you running from, darlin'?" he asked with real concern. "You tell me who's making you work, I'll arrest them *right now.*"

Not if she pays you off, Eva thought bitterly.

The officer made the mistake of letting go of her shoulders while holding tight to the curtain. In a moment she was free, running again, the night air chilling her bare arms and legs. A few shouts followed her down the street, but she ducked into a darkened alleyway and slid behind a pile of stinking garbage. There she crouched, shivering, trying to quiet her gasping breath.

Footsteps came near, tramped in a circle, stopped. "Damn. She's gone," came the officer's voice. The footsteps faded away.

Eva kept to the alleys. She crossed the street once and was met with jeers, but no one chased her. She reached Mr. Stonewall's door and pounded on it with both fists. Her feet burned like fire on the frozen ground. A groggy voice from inside called, "Who's that?"

But Eva couldn't say her name. This was not her, running half naked through the streets. It could not be her. "Mr. Stonewall!" she cried. "Open up! Please!"

Mr. Stonewall must have recognized her voice. He swung open the door, and Eva stumbled inside. "Lord," he said. "Oh, Lord." He threw a blanket around Eva's shoulders and pulled her to the warm stove.

"What have they done to you, Miss Eva?" Mr. Stonewall asked, his eyes filling with tears. "What have they done?"

Eva let the tears fall now. She hunched over, pulling the blanket tight around her, and leaned close to the stove to soak in its warmth.

Mr. Stonewall patted her shoulder gingerly. "You're all right now, Miss Eva," he was saying. "You're safe."

Eva nodded. "I'm all right." *No harm done,* she thought, *just a sprained ankle and bruised feet.* "I ran away before . . ." Before it could get any worse. Could she tell him how bad it had been? How she couldn't even face herself each evening?

"You done a brave thing, Miss Eva," Mr. Stonewall said.

"I should have done it sooner," she said miserably. Then she poured it all out, about the dance hall, the men, the debts, and even the food—how she'd never seen so much good food in her life and how she was afraid that if she left Miss B's house, she'd be hungry again like last winter. . . .

Mr. Stonewall shook his head. "Miss Eva, don't blame yourself. You ain't been given an easy hand to play."

Suddenly Eva remembered: a police officer had seen her. There would be questions asked. She'd still been close to Miss B's house when the officer grabbed her. If the questioning reached Miss B and someone had seen Eva enter Mr.

Stonewall's house . . . She knew enough about how justice was paid out to black folks to know she couldn't stay here, not even until morning.

"I have to go," she said urgently. "I have to take the train to Georgetown."

"What's in Georgetown?" Mr. Stonewall asked.

"Mrs. Santini, our old neighbor, and her husband. I think they'll help me."

Mr. Stonewall went to an old wooden crate. It opened with a creak. He pulled out a maroon gingham dress and let out a heavy sigh. "Probably should have given this to the church a long time ago," he said, "but I liked having something of hers around." His eyes seemed to focus far away, on a memory. Then he snapped back to the present. "It'll be big—she was more stout than you—but it'll do." He handed the dress to Eva, then bent over the chest again to pull out a woolen shawl, a pair of black wool stockings, and worn high-button shoes.

Eva held the dress and just looked at it. "Wear your Alice's clothes?" she asked, incredulous. "But they're your *memories*."

"I can remember my Alice without her old dress in this trunk. My memories are in *here*." He tapped his chest.

"I'll send them back," Eva said. "I promise."

Eva took the clothes and went behind the dressing screen. She pulled the dress over her head and buttoned up the bodice.

Then she took the shawl and wrapped it snugly around her shoulders, pulled on the stockings, and slipped her feet into the sturdy shoes. They were large, but nothing a few wads of newspaper couldn't remedy. When she came out, Mr. Stonewall nodded approvingly.

"Now, one more thing," he said. "You need money for the train ticket and for food when you get there. And what if this Mrs. Santini ain't there? If she's not, then you'll need money for the train ticket home." He took a knife and pried up a section of a floorboard. From under it he retrieved a small sack of coins. "I was saving this so I don't end up being buried in a field for poor folks—wanted a real headstone next to Alice's, you know?" He counted out the coins, put them into Eva's hand, and closed her fingers around them. "But once I'm dead, it won't hardly matter, and you're still alive, so I think you can make better use."

"But I've got some money," Eva said. "A silver dollar." She wanted to tell him that there was no way in creation she was coming back, so a return ticket would not be necessary, but she held her tongue.

Mr. Stonewall shook his head. "Tell you what. I ain't fixing to die anytime soon, so if you've still got that silver dollar once you get yourself settled, you go ahead and mail me back some money. But in the meantime you keep it, in case what I've given you ain't enough."

To herself, Eva swore she would mail back the clothes and the money. It was the only way she could bring herself to take them now.

Mr. Stonewall pointed one finger in the air, as if he'd just remembered something. From the bread box he pulled out biscuits wrapped in a rag. "Don't waste your money on none of that food the butcher comes to sell on the train," he said. Then from a hook on the wall he took down a metal canteen. "Once you get up in those mountains, you get powerful thirsty." He used the dipper to fill the canteen. "And don't be trying to drink from the dipper on the train. Some white folks'll sooner shoot you than let you drink from their water crock." He handed the canteen to her. "Now you get some sleep, and I'll sit up," he said. "Come daylight, I'll walk you to the train station."

"No!" Eva objected. "I have to go *now*. A policeman saw me. What if Miss B tries to put the blame on you to keep it off her?"

"Oh, Lord." Mr. Stonewall rubbed his forehead.

"I know my way to the train station," Eva said. "I'll be fine."

"You can't get to Georgetown from the Kansas Pacific station," he said. "Those big railroad men couldn't see fit to get along, so they built a different station for most every rail line coming into this town. You need the Colorado Central depot down on Delgany Street. I'll walk you there."

"But what if someone sees you? That Miss B is ruthless!" Eva objected.

Mr. Stonewall was already putting on his hat and coat. "Then you'd better send back my money in a hurry, because I *do* want a decent burial." He chuckled, but Eva didn't think it was funny, and she let him know so with a deep frown.

"Here," he said. He took one last item out of the wooden chest: a lady's fancy hat, with a wide brim and a feather. "Pull this down over your face. Anybody sees us, they'll think I'm walking with my Alice's ghost. They'll scream and run the other way, and we'll stroll on along like nothing happened."

Eva smiled. "And I'll give you back the hat once we reach the station," she said. She was glad he would be keeping at least one memento of his dead wife.

"Fair enough," said Mr. Stonewall.

The night air felt cold on Eva's cheeks, but she was warm in Miss Alice's clothes. The gas streetlights gave off a friendly glow. Eva took Mr. Stonewall's arm. "Thank you so very much," she said.

"You keep yourself safe—that's the thanks I want," he said. "Write me a letter to tell me that Eye-talian friend of yours is taking good care of you. That'll make me happy."

"Will you tell Mrs. Boyd and the folks at church good-bye for me?" Eva asked. She had wanted to go back to church with him, to go every week and become part of that warm, welcoming community.

"I surely will," Mr. Stonewall promised.

The Colorado Central depot was a simple wooden building. Mr. Stonewall offered to sit and wait with her, but they both knew it would be too risky for him to be seen with her, given the circumstances. Eva told him to go home and get some sleep.

She tried not to think about the fact that she would probably never see him again. "I will write to you," she said, and her voice caught in her throat.

Mr. Stonewall patted her cheek, his eyes sad.

Eva tried to brighten the mood for both of them. "Maybe I can come visit you when I'm all grown-up. I'll save my pennies so I can."

"That'll be right fine," said Mr. Stonewall. "I'll look forward to your visit."

She gave him back the hat and stood on tiptoes to give him a kiss on the cheek. Then she kept her eyes cast down as he walked away so she wouldn't have to watch.

Eva took a seat on a cold wooden bench. The station was quiet except for the night watchman making his rounds. "Mama Kate," Eva whispered. "I know I haven't been making you glad these last weeks . . . but I'm fixing to do better now. I hope you think it's a good thing that I'm going to Mrs. Santini's, and I hope she'll let me stay with her, and I hope I can find a job so that I won't be a burden and so I can send Mr. Stonewall's money back to him and send money back to Miss B so she won't put Sadie in jail because of my debts. . . . Mama Kate, you always said that the Lord never gives us more burdens than we can carry, but right now I feel like I'm carrying about enough to break my shoulders." She shook her head, slumping in her seat. "But I'm not broken yet, so I guess I'll keep on." She pulled the shawl up over her head and waited for the first morning train to Golden, Forks Creek, Idaho Springs, and finally to Georgetown.

Eva had meant to sit up until dawn, so when she was jostled awake by a man plopping down next to her on the bench, she was surprised to find that her head had drooped in sleep. The man opened his newspaper, the *Denver Times*, and ignored her. All around her, the station was coming alive with the bustle of passengers arriving for the early morning trains. Eva jumped up to go to the ticket window. She adjusted the shawl on her head and wrapped it under her chin. She didn't want to go around bareheaded in public, and it was the only hat she had.

As she stepped up to the ticket window, the ticket seller peered at her through the bars. "Just off the boat, eh?" he said. Then he addressed a man at a desk behind him. "There's more and more of them every day—don't speak a word of English, but they want jobs." To Eva he barked loudly, "Where are you going? What *town*?"

"Georgetown," she said, uncomfortable being stared at by the men behind the counter.

"She's a pretty one. I know where she can get a job!" said the ticket seller, and both men guffawed.

Eva glared menacingly at them as she snatched her ticket off the counter.

"Uh-oh. I think she understood!" More laughter.

Eva realized that with her features and coloring, which could easily look foreign, her too-big dress, and the shawl over her head, these men had mistaken her for a European immigrant. She was about to tell them they were ignorant brutes and should shut their mouths, but the man behind her in line pushed her out of the way so he could buy his ticket.

She didn't have long to wait for the train. When she went to step up into the car, the conductor stopped her.

"Miss, where are your bags?" he demanded.

Eva clutched the small sack with the coins, biscuits, and canteen inside. It was all she had. She didn't know what to say. Should she lie and say that her aunt had taken her bags yesterday and would be meeting her in Georgetown?

The conductor raised his voice to a shout, the way people did when speaking to foreigners, as if the volume would make them more easily understood. *"Where are your bags?"* he yelled, hurting her ears.

Eva decided to play things to her advantage. She held up her little sack and shook her head, then climbed the steps past him into the train car.

"Wretched thing," she heard him say as she passed. "They come here hoping to find a better life, and they're just as dirt-poor as ever. And they bring all their lice with them."

As a man stepped up behind her, the conductor warned him,

"I'd sit far from that one if I were you. Her head is probably crawling with lice under that shawl."

Perfect, thought Eva. *No one will sit next to me, no one will bother me.* Just to make sure, she reached up and scratched her head.

As the train left the station, the sun was just hitting the tops of the snow-covered mountains, lighting them with an orange glow. Her stomach tensed. What was she doing going up *into* those monsters? How could anyone live where the land sat sideways instead of lying flat like it was supposed to? She squinted at the shining mountains. All right, she thought, calming herself, if Mrs. Santini could live up there, then so could she.

The train chugged past the last of the flat, familiar plains, past the straw-colored buffalo grass and green tufts of soap weed. Then it raced toward the foothills as if it would crash into them and kill everyone on board.

The conductor fed coal into the potbellied stove at the end of the car, and coal smoke filled the air. Eva coughed, then took a drink from the canteen. She noted the stone crock near the coal stove, with a dipper hooked to its edge—something she hadn't noticed on her first train ride. She would not drink from the dipper, even if these people thought she was European rather than colored, but she could refill the canteen with it. She took out one of the biscuits and nibbled at it.

As they neared the mountains, brown, flat-topped hills filled her view, and the bigger mountains disappeared behind them. The train stopped in Golden, then climbed higher up the hills, slowing as the track rose steeply.

They entered a narrow canyon. A stream ran alongside the tracks, tumbling green and white down its course. She heard the man behind her tell his companion, "This here's Clear Creek Canyon. That Clear Creek is mighty good fishing."

The narrow-gauge railroad track wound its way up the canyon, following Clear Creek with all its twists and turns. Again and again, the train approached a steep cliff of salmon-colored rock only to turn at the last moment before slamming into it. Eva held the arms of her seat so tightly her knuckles hurt. She could see the rock rushing by just inches from her window. Jagged cliffs loomed high above her, with stands of dark pines clinging to the edges. She felt breathless at the speed of it, the beauty of it.

The train stopped in Forks Creek to take on water for the steam engine from a large, round water tank. A man came on board selling sandwiches, fruit, and newspapers, walking through the cars, calling out his wares. Eva was glad she didn't have to spend her money on his expensive goods.

The train continued on its way. Now that Eva was convinced they would not crash into a cliff side, she began to enjoy watching the splendor unfold around her. Her ears popped as the train climbed. She used the edge of her shawl to rub a clearer spot on the window and was dismayed when the shawl came away black with coal soot. When the conductor called out, "Georgetown. End of the line. All passengers unload at Georgetown!" she was actually disappointed that the ride was over.

Eva left the train station and followed the flow of passengers walking down Rose Street past a collection of one- and two-story frame houses. She assumed they were headed toward the heart of town, where she expected to find the post office. The postman would be able to tell her where the Santinis lived. As she walked, she thought about what Sadie and Pearl might be doing. She hoped they were all right. She wondered if Sadie was arguing with Miss B again or if Pearl was sharpening her fingernails for self-protection. An image flashed in her mind of two uniformed police officers handcuffing Sadie and Pearl, leading them away to jail, and Pearl cussing and yelling, "This is *her* fault! She run off without paying!" Eva groaned. She promised herself anew that she would send back money just as soon as she could.

Georgetown's 6th Street looked to be the town's center, with shops, saloons, and hotels lining each side and almost as many horses, carts, and pedestrians as a busy street in Denver. At either end of 6th Street, steep, towering mountains rose: Georgetown was crowded into a hollow with the mountains themselves dictating just how far the town could spread.

Eva stopped in a dry goods store to buy a square of tan cotton cloth, which she folded diagonally, draped over her head, and tied under her chin like a kerchief. It cost much less than a hat and left her shawl free to wrap around her shoulders against the crisp, cold mountain air. Besides, she was pleased with the distance people afforded her when they thought she was an immigrant and didn't speak English. She'd rather not be questioned: Why was she traveling alone? Where were her kinfolk? She'd rather not be bothered.

At the post office she said simply, "Signora Santini?"

The postmaster was a stout man with a head of thick, curly red hair. A scrawny young boy, about eleven years old, with the same ruddy hair, stood at the counter, sorting mail. The postmaster called to the boy.

"She's looking for Santini. Is that the nice lady used to come in here sometimes with a letter to Italy? Haven't seen her for a couple of weeks now. You know where she went, son?"

The boy shook his head. He was concentrating intently on the envelope in his hand, his lips moving as he read the name written there.

The postmaster frowned. "Ain't you learned to read yet? What kind of help can you be if you can't read no faster than a turtle?"

"I'm getting it, Papa. Just give me a minute," the boy whined.

Eva noticed that the postmaster himself did not take over

the job and guessed that as poor as his son was at reading, the father most likely was worse.

The postmaster turned to Eva and shouted as if to make himself understood in English. "No Santini. No. No Santini here."

Eva left, her ears ringing and her heart sunk down to her toes.

The sound of rushing water reminded Eva of her thirst. She would get a drink, then figure out what to do.

The creek ran right through Georgetown, gurgling between the unpainted houses as if a mere town could not deter it on its mad rush down the mountain. The water was icy cold and sweet tasting. Eva washed her face and hands, took a long drink, and filled the canteen. Then she sat on a rock in the sun to think.

To go back to Denver was out of the question. But where had the Santinis *gone?* Surely not back to Italy. Had they moved to another town? With dismay she remembered that Georgetown was the end of the railroad line. If they'd moved farther into the mountains, she had no way of getting there. Her stomach growled. It had been hours since she finished the biscuits. How long would Mr. Stonewall's money hold out, especially now that she had to pay for a place to sleep? She'd already seen that there was lodging available at several hotels—Barton House and Hotel de Paris—but at what cost? Though Georgetown had its share of saloons and scruffy-looking miners in the streets, she could see that it also had fine houses and an air of luxury. She had heard that in mining boomtowns, prices for even simple things, like a loaf of bread, could be sky-high. Mr. Stonewall's money *and* her silver dollar would be gone in no time if she tried to stay here.

She looked down into the stream. "Mama Kate," she said. "I'm stuck. Stuck and alone, and I don't have much money, and if you didn't think it was a good idea for me to come find Mrs. Santini, I wish you'd have *told* me." She rested her chin on her knees. "It's fine that you listen, but I'm tired of not being able to hear what you think is best for me. What am I supposed to *do*?"

"Miss?" A small voice came from behind her.

Eva swung around to find the redheaded boy from the post office staring at her. The sound of the rushing stream must have covered his footsteps. "Who are you talking to?" he asked, cocking his head.

Eva felt her cheeks flush. "Myself," she said crossly. "Sometimes when I'm thinking, I talk to myself. What do you want?"

The boy fidgeted with his shirttail, one side of which was hanging out. "Papa said to find you," he said. "He remembers now that Mrs. Santini and her husband were heading to Silver Plume. They'd heard there are lots of Italians there and the mining is going full steam. And . . . ." The boy's face turned strawberry red and his words came out in a rush. "He says you're too pretty to be alone in this town and I'm to bring you home to my ma. Emilio, the Portuguese, he takes the mail and train deliveries up the toll road to Silver Plume every day, and he can get you there safe. You can go tomorrow."

Eva jumped to her feet. "*Thank* you," she said, hoping that her sincerity would make up for her earlier rudeness. Then she closed her eyes for just long enough to say silently, *Thank you, Mama Kate, for watching over me.* She opened her eyes and smiled at the boy.

He looked at her hard. "You don't talk funny like Mrs. Santini," he said.

Eva was about to explain that she was not, in fact, Mrs. Santini's kin. Then she hesitated. If they didn't see her as Italian, would they then see that she was colored? Would this boy's family still invite her for supper and to stay the night if they knew she was colored? There were opinionated people in every town; this she was sure of. She quickly made the decision: it would be safer to let them go on thinking she was Mrs. Santini's kin. "I just speak English better than Mrs. Santini does," she said.

The boy laughed. "Dad thinks you can *only* talk Italian. He told me how I'd have to point to things, and if I couldn't get you to understand about coming to our house, he said I should take your hand and haul you there. It'll be a big laugh when he finds out he was wrong!" He frowned a bit. "Though he'll be mad. My dad, he doesn't like to be wrong."

"Maybe we shouldn't tell him," Eva blurted out. Her heart raced. She couldn't jeopardize this chance for a meal and a place to stay and a ride to Silver Plume. The safest thing would be to play the role of new immigrant. "I'll be leaving in the morning, so it'll just be for one night." She gave him a pleading look. "Can we keep it a secret? Please?"

The boy nodded enthusiastically. "That'll be a good secret, Dad being wrong and only you and me knowing that he's wrong." He grinned at the thought of it. They traded introductions— his name was William Flanagan—and he led the way to his house.

William's home was one of the small, one-story frame houses, with a stand of pine trees protecting its western side from wind and storms. William's mother was a worn-out-looking woman with her hair pulled back tightly in a bun and the white lace collar on her dress dirty with wear. As she prepared supper, she chatted in her Irish brogue, asking Eva loads of questions but never waiting for an answer, so that Eva wasn't quite sure if her husband had told her about the language "problem" or not. William sat at the kitchen table, listening. He seemed to be enjoying the excitement of having a houseguest and of keeping a secret.

When William's father came home, there was a rush to get supper on the table, one moment of quiet during grace, and then a very noisy meal, with Mr. and Mrs. Flanagan doing all of the talking.

First Mrs. Flanagan started. "So, Mrs. Santini is your kin? The boat trip across the ocean on that crowded ship, was it wretched? Believe me, I remember. How do you like it here in America?"

But William's father broke in. "Don't ask her so many questions. She doesn't understand you anyway. How is she supposed to answer, in *Italian*?"

"She understands. She went right to the privy when I told her where it was. You understand, don't you, dear?"

"Don't bother the poor girl—can't you see she's trying to eat? She's probably had nothing but cold bread for days. And God knows what they had to eat in that poor country of hers."

"I'm not bothering her, I'm just trying to make her feel at home. . . ."

For a moment there was silence as they all chewed. Then Mr. Flanagan held up a fork full of stew, widened his eyes, pointed to it, and said loudly, "Good?" Then, rubbing his fat belly, "Mmmmm." Pointing again, "Good? You like?"

But Mrs. Flanagan butted in. "Don't embarrass her, Frank. What if she doesn't like it? What is she supposed to say? I'm sure it's all different from what she's used to."

"I can try to make conversation, can't I? What's the harm

in that? She's going to have to learn a few words in English, anyway."

"It's not polite to *ask* if she likes it. Folks will tell you if they like your cooking."

"How is she supposed to tell you when she can't speak a word of English? Huh? Do you mind telling me that?"

And on it went. Eva could see William desperately trying not to laugh. She knew she dare not speak a word of English now.

At bedtime, Mrs. Flanagan made up a cot for Eva in a corner of the one bedroom the family shared. Eva showed her appreciation with smiles, nods, and a kiss gently planted on the kind woman's cheek.

The next morning, carrying a small sack filled with apples, cold meat, and bread, Eva walked with Mr. Flanagan to the livery stable near the train depot. They went around back, where two men were loading goods onto a buckboard. Two sullen-looking horses stood nearby. One of the men was dark, with a black mustache—Eva took him to be the Portuguese—and one had hair so white blond and skin so red that Eva had to stop herself from staring at the strangeness of it. As Eva and the postmaster approached, the men stopped working, took off their hats, and nodded their hellos.

"Emilio." The postmaster addressed the man with the black mustache. "I want you to take this young lady to Silver Plume when you take the mail."

"I would be happy to." Emilio grinned and wiggled his eyebrows at Eva.

"And be polite to her," the postmaster snapped. "She's kin to Mrs. Santini. She's on her way to find her."

Emilio's grin softened to a friendly smile. "We will take her soon as we're done loading." His accent was melodious, and it reminded her of Carlos.

"She speaks only Italian, no English," said the postmaster.

"That's okay. Anders here speaks only Swedish, but we get along fine," said Emilio, laughing.

Eva didn't want Mr. Flanagan to leave without her having a chance to thank him, so she used one of the Italian words she'd learned from Mrs. Santini. "*Grazie,*" she said, taking his hand.

"What's she want?" the postmaster asked.

"She's thanking you," said Emilio. "Somebody taught her manners."

"Ah, you're welcome," the postmaster said loudly to Eva. Then he handed a sack of mail to Emilio and left.

Eva took a seat and watched as the buckboard was piled higher with goods: sacks of grain, crates marked THIS SIDE UP, barrels, the bag of mail. She guessed that this was the way food, coal, cloth, and everything else people needed were carried from the train depot in Georgetown to the town of Silver Plume, higher up the mountain.

Suddenly Emilio let out a belly laugh, then a whoop. "We hit the jackpot!" He held up a large jug of whiskey. "I don't think nobody in Silver Plume will miss this, do you?"

The Swede might not have understood English, but he understood what was in the bottle and what Emilio meant to do with it. They settled in together on a low bench in the morning sun, passing the jug and swigging happily.

Eva fidgeted impatiently. She grew hungry, took out an apple, and ate it, then scuffed her shoes in the dirt. How long would it take them to finish the jug? And what kind of shape would they be in once they *had* finished it? She looked at the horses, standing still except for their ears twitching and their tails swishing away flies, and thought she must look as sullen and long faced as they did.

The sun crept higher into the sky, warming the cool mountain air. When the jug was empty, the men leaned back against the stable wall and closed their eyes. Eva's patience ran out.

She stomped over and nudged Emilio with her foot. "When are we leaving?" she demanded. She figured he was too drunk to remember it if she spoke a little English.

Emilio stirred, blinked up at her as if trying to remember who she was, then straightened. "Aw, we can still get there today. Only takes a couple hours—it's just a few miles up the Plume Hill road." He waved a limp hand in the direction of a wagon road that zigzagged up out of town, then leveled off and skirted the mountainside until it disappeared from sight.

"Tomorrow at the latest," he said, and leaned his head against the wall again. Then, eyes closed, he mumbled to himself, "Her English isn't half bad."

Tomorrow?! Eva stared at the dozing men in despair. Where was she supposed to sleep? And what if they found another jug of whiskey tomorrow morning? Or if they felt so rotten tomorrow, they decided to wait yet another day? She looked up at the Plume Hill road. There could only be one road, she thought. She couldn't get lost. And it was only a few miles. She might have to pay the toll, but she had coins for that. She had food, good sturdy shoes, the canteen filled with fresh water, and enough daylight to easily get to Silver Plume before dark. She took one last look at the dozing men and started toward the road to Silver Plume.

The wagon road rose steeply at first and brought Eva to where she could look down at all of Georgetown. Rows of houses were clustered in the center of town and spread outward from there to the stragglers perched where the mountains began to rise. The height made her dizzy, and she clutched a boulder for support. Across the valley, almost in her face, was another mountain of gray and orange cliffs and scree sprinkled with a few pines the loggers had missed. She thought back to the comfortable, predictable flatness of the plains, of home. She never would have guessed that there were places where the earth rose straight up.

As she walked, Eva found herself easily out of breath and remembered that Mr. Stonewall had warned her about the air being "thinner" up here in the mountains. Just before the road leveled out, it passed directly in front of a two-story brick house. A woman sat on the porch in a rocking chair, a pile of knitting in her lap. *This must be the tollhouse,* Eva thought. She began to step up onto the porch to ask how much she had to pay, but the woman waved her on. "No charge for walkers," she called out. Eva nodded and continued on her way.

Farther up the road, Eva stopped to gaze around her. The

beauty was overwhelming. She breathed deeply. She felt peaceful and free: Miss B could not find her here, nor could a nosy policeman or a grumpy train conductor worried about lice. And here she could not bring trouble to Mr. Stonewall nor to William's kind family. She pulled her kerchief forward so that it shaded her eyes from the bright sun. She even felt closer to Mama Kate and Daddy Walter here—up here closer to heaven.

Her reverie was interrupted by the clop-clopping of hooves on the road behind her. Lord, she thought, was this the drunken Emilio coming up to Silver Plume today after all? She decided she'd rather walk the rest of the way herself and quickly trotted down a steep foot trail toward a stand of pines on the mountainside below.

It was chilly in the shade of the pines, but she was well hidden from the road. She listened as the wagon passed by. Her stomach grumbled for lunch, and she figured this was a good place to stop to eat. She pulled out the bread and a chunk of pork wrapped in greasy paper. It smelled delicious. As she sat eating and taking sips of water from the canteen, she heard a soft scrabbling on the rocks behind her. She turned to see what was there. A red fox startled, ran a few paces back up the mountain, then stopped and looked directly at her, his eyes round and intelligent.

"You sniffed out my lunch, didn't you?" she said.

The fox blinked but didn't move.

"I can share," Eva said. She placed a piece of meat on the rock, then moved away and stood very still.

The fox waited, watching. Suddenly he scrambled down the hillside, jumped onto the rock, and ate the meat in one gulp. Licking his mouth, he looked up at her.

"You want more, do you?" Eva asked, laughing. But she shook her head. "I need to save the rest for *me.*"

She promised herself that as soon as she got settled in Silver Plume with work and food and a place to live, she would come back to this spot and share another meal with the friendly fox. She gathered the remains of her lunch and began to hike back up the steep path toward the wagon road. The beauty of the sunlit mountainside lifted her spirits, and she began to sing. Perhaps that was why she did not hear the soft padding of heavy paws behind her. Or maybe it was because the mountain lion was a very quiet stalker.

The smell caught Eva's attention first. It wafted to her on the breeze: the gamy odor of male cat. The small hairs on the back of her neck prickled and she wheeled around. There it was, so close: yellow eyes, a massive head, lowered, ready to pounce, then a flash of sunlight on tawny fur as the cat leaped. Eva screamed, raised her arms to block the blow. The cat's full weight shocked her body. She fell back, rolled down the mountainside, the huge cat bounding after her. She hit a boulder, jerked to a stop. The mountain lion raked her neck, its claws digging deep. "No!" Eva shrieked, the pain awakening rage. She jumped to her feet, ran. The paws thudded into her back, knocked her forward, down. She cried out, twisted under the cat's weight.

Four long yellow fangs hovered above her face, then lowered and sank into the flesh of her scalp. "Noooo!" Too much pain. She heard the horrible, hollow scraping of the beast's teeth against her skull. She clutched wildly at the cat's head, grasping, pushing. Her thumb touched something wet and soft. With all the rage inside her she shoved her thumb deep into the cat's eye socket.

The mountain lion squalled, let go its hold. Eva rolled, somehow found her footing, ran. Blood streamed down her face, her neck, soaked into her clothes. She stumbled, kept running, down, away. She heard a bird call, sharp and shrill. There was one last flash of sunlight, then her vision darkened and she felt the hard edges of rock as she fell.

She would always think of it later as simply The Dream. There was no pain, no fear, only a soft light that seemed to wrap her in its warmth. Mama Kate was there and Daddy Walter, too, holding her, whispering to her, not with words exactly, but with love. And she knew, *knew* in her bones, that they loved her, would always love her, even when she thought she had done wrong, even when she was the most disgusted with herself, even when she was in despair of ever finding her way again. There was light and love and comfort until the whisperings turned into farewells, and the soft light grew to a glaring, hurting brightness, and she was slammed back into the pain, her head throbbing, her neck on fire.

It felt as if someone was washing her wounds very gently. She tried to open her eyes, but sunlight stabbed them. "Who's there?" she asked, her words slurred with grogginess. No answer. The washing continued. She faded back into unconsciousness.

Was it hours later? Days? The sunlight had softened. She heard hooves scraping against rocks, footsteps, a man's voice. "Ah, God, she's dead."

"Scat. Get away from her." A boy's voice. Was it William? "Papa, why won't that fox leave her?"

Strong arms slid under her knees, behind her shoulders, lifted her. The movement awakened pain. She groaned.

"She's alive!" Mr. Flanagan's voice. "William, help me get her onto the mule." Mr. Flanagan mounted the mule, still holding her. "Damn them. Damn *me.* I never should have trusted them with her. I'll rot in hell's flames for this for sure."

Eva felt the rocking gait as the mule picked its way up the steep path toward the wagon road. As the pain grew to a crescendo, she felt herself slipping back into unconsciousness. The last thing she heard was William saying, "Papa, that fox is following us," and Mr. Flanagan's answer, "He'll stop before we get to town."

"Frank, I don't think she is who she says she is." Mrs. Flanagan's voice was hushed. She sounded curious but not unkind. "She's been moaning and mumbling when I change her bandages, and sometimes she says out-and-out words, and . . . well, she doesn't sound Italian at all. She sounds like a proper American if you ask me. And you know as well as I do she looks like she's colored. So if she told you she was kin of Mrs. Santini's and just off the boat from Italy, she was making up a story."

"How could she have made up a story to tell me when she

doesn't speak a word of English?" Mr. Flanagan demanded. "And I heard her speak Italian. She said thank you to me plain as day, 'grassy' or something like that, and Emilio had to translate. And don't they have colored folks in Italy, same as here?"

"Frank, I'm telling you, the girl is no immigrant. I don't know *who* she is or what we're going to do with her when she gets well, but I heard her say, 'Ow, that hurts,' and when I told her it's doctor's orders, she said, 'All right.' And sometimes she mumbles something about 'Mama Kate.' "

"Well, it doesn't matter whether she *is* Mrs. Santini's kin now anyway. Emilio just brought back word from the postmaster in Silver Plume: the Santinis moved on to Leadville already. Would *you* send a young girl all those miles to Leadville on her own? And who's going to pay the stagecoach fare? Besides, with all the drunken fighting and murdering that goes on in that town, it's no place for her to be wandering around trying to find Mrs. Santini. That woman can come *here* to get her—that's what I say. I'm not putting this girl in harm's way again."

"I'm telling you, I don't think she's Mrs. Santini's kin. . . ."

Eva lay on her cot, listening to this conversation, and decided it was time the Flanagans knew the truth. She still felt weak, but she raised herself up on one elbow. "Mr. and Mrs. Flanagan," she called, but it came out no more than a whisper. She cleared her throat. "Please," she said as loudly as she could.

Mr. and Mrs. Flanagan came to her, their faces hopeful. "Are you feeling better, child?" Mrs. Flanagan asked.

"Yes," Eva said, then she looked right at Mr. Flanagan. "I'm so sorry for making you believe I spoke only Italian. It started as an accident, and then I thought you'd be angry. . . ."

Mr. Flanagan dropped to one knee beside her bed. "I've got so much guilt in here"—he punched his fist against his chest— "for what happened to you, there's no room for anger, I can tell you that. I'm just glad you're alive."

Eva shook her head. "It's not your fault. I shouldn't have left the wagon road—"

"Stop this now," Mrs. Flanagan interrupted her. "No one is to blame except whatever it was got you. Doc Pollock thought it was a young mountain lion. Was he right?"

Eva nodded and winced a bit.

Mr. Flanagan whistled. "What scared it off?" he asked.

Eva remembered the feel of finding the cat's eye socket, of shoving her thumb deep, and the sound of the cat's squall as it let go. "I did," she said.

Mr. Flanagan raised his eyebrows and dropped his jaw in amazement.

"But how did you find me?" Eva asked.

"Ah, that scoundrel Emilio," Mr. Flanagan said. "I went to check that he'd delivered you safely and found him drunker than a cowhand on payday. William said maybe you'd walked, so we started up the road. We found out you'd passed the tollhouse, so we kept going. When I saw you lying on the rocks down below, I thought you were dead for sure."

Mrs. Flanagan patted Eva's cheek. "Thank goodness you found her when you did," she said. "I'll go fix supper now. You look well enough to join us at the table today, dear. You can tell us all about yourself."

Eva tried to smile but thought it must have looked more like a grimace. "That sounds good," she said stiffly.

When the Flanagans had left her alone, she dove under her pillow. "Lord, Mama Kate, what do I do *now*? If I tell them about Sadie and Miss B's and dancing, they're sure to kick me out— respectable people don't want to associate with the likes of folks at Miss B's. But I need time to get a letter to Mrs. Santini and hear back from her." She sighed. "I hate to do this, Mama Kate, but I'm going to have to lie to these good people. It'll be a small lie—just enough to make it so they'll let me stay." She sat up, swung her legs over the side of the bed, and waited for the dizziness to pass. "Mama Kate, remember when you used to say my hands were as strong as any man's from scrubbing heavy linens and dungarees all day?" She smiled proudly. "Well, I think you were right—at least that mountain lion seemed to think so."

At supper Eva told the Flanagans about her mother and sister in Denver who were sick and had sent her to live with Mrs.

chapter eighteen

Santini until they got well. She asked for paper and pen so she could write to Mrs. Santini in Leadville. Mr. Flanagan said he'd make sure the letter was sent on the stagecoach in the morning.

Eva didn't know if Mrs. Santini was still in Leadville, if she would write back, if she'd let her come live with her, or if she'd be able to send money for her stagecoach fare. But while Eva waited to hear, she had a bed and food, time for her wounds to heal, and hope.

By the end of her first week of living with the Flanagans, Eva was up and around and helping with chores. Mrs. Flanagan had washed Eva's shawl and dress—the bloodstains hardly showed on the maroon gingham—and neatly repaired the rips. Eva now did the washing and cooking alongside Mrs. Flanagan and went to the post office each day to sort mail. She helped William with his lessons—he was particularly slow in reading—and quizzed him on his memorization of American presidents, from George Washington right up to Rutherford B. Hayes. At meals she ate only small portions so as not to be a burden.

Eva checked the post each day for a letter from Mrs. Santini, but she didn't feel disappointed when none arrived. She'd be glad to stay with the Flanagans all winter, if it came to that. It felt so good to be living in a normal household again—to go to bed early and wake with the sun, to roll up her sleeves and scrub floors or knead dough for bread. Mrs. Flanagan often sent her down to 6th Street to do the marketing. Eva liked to go into Mr. Cohen's C.O.D. store, which sold just about everything, and look at the tall shelves stacked with goods. When she passed by Mr. Townsend's barbershop, if he happened to be out front sweeping the sidewalk, he gave her a special hello, which she suspected was because he was colored, too. And she liked looking up at the mountainside just after dark, when the night-shift miners were on their way to the Lebanon Mine and their lanterns looked like so many fireflies, bobbing as they walked.

After two weeks, Doc Pollock came to take out her stitches. Eva shut her eyes tight, gripped the chair edge, and managed not to cry. The doctor gave her a pat on the shoulder when it was all over.

"I figure it must have been a young one that attacked you," he said, putting away his scissors and tweezers. "If it had been full grown, it would have dragged you off for supper."

Eva shivered, but Mrs. Flanagan distracted her by fussing with her hair. "We'll cut some bangs, and no one will be able to see your scars at all. You'll be good as new!" she said brightly.

That night in bed, with Mr. and Mrs. Flanagan still in the kitchen and William already asleep in his bed, Eva whispered to Mama Kate, "This is a good place, Mama Kate. These are good people, and it feels like a real home, a lot the way our home used to be. I could stay here . . . maybe forever." As she drifted off to sleep, she felt thankful and safe. And so when whispering woke her later that night, she was shocked by what she heard.

"I had to do it," Mr. Flanagan said. "What with the doc needing to be paid, we'll all go hungry soon if we keep trying to feed the four of us. But I did *not* do it because of the tongue waggers, even though they've got a point about a girl and a boy not kin sleeping in the same room."

"I know, Frank," Mrs. Flanagan said. "I just hope those gossips don't think they're getting their way—threatening your job because you've got a colored girl under your roof. They've got no right."

"No, they've got no right," said Mr. Flanagan.

"When will we tell her?" Mrs. Flanagan asked.

"The sooner the better, before she gets too settled in here. You know as well as I do those Santinis won't have the money to pay her stagecoach fare to Leadville—not on a miner's wages, they won't. No sense waiting for a letter from them." Mr. Flanagan sighed heavily. "I guess we'll tell her tomorrow."

Eva barely slept the rest of the night, waiting for what she would hear come morning.

"If we could keep you here with us, we would." Mrs. Flanagan took Eva's hands in hers. "But there just isn't enough to go around, and with winter coming . . ."

Mr. Flanagan looked down at his feet. "We felt it was best," he said woodenly.

"It'll be just until your mother and sister are well again, and then you'll be right there in Denver, so it will be easy for you to get home," Mrs. Flanagan said. "If you were up in Leadville, you'd be so very far away."

"But when we get a letter from Mrs. Santini, we'll send it right to you," Mr. Flanagan promised.

Eva now held the letter that spelled out her future:

Dear Mr. Flanagan,

Have received your inquiry regarding girl, age thirteen. We do have room, as we need older children to help with so many little ones. Write to tell me when arriving and I will meet her at the train station.

Yours truly,
Mrs. Matilda Hinsley
Denver Orphans' Home

The morning Eva left Georgetown, snow had begun to fall. It dusted the rooftops and blue spruce trees, making the town look like a Christmas picture even though it was only October.

Eva wore her kerchief around her neck and one of Mrs. Flanagan's old hats. Along with newly cut bangs, the kerchief and hat neatly concealed her scabs and scars. Mrs. Flanagan sat with Eva on a train station bench and fidgeted with the string on a package of food she'd made up. "Now you've got cold chicken, bread, a tin of crackers, and a jar of peaches. You never know how long these train trips will take. What if the snow builds up on the tracks and you have to wait overnight to get plowed out? Or if it's a blizzard and you're stuck for days?"

"Thank you," said Eva. "Thank you for *everything*. I'll send money for my doctor's bills when I can."

"Don't you worry about that," Mrs. Flanagan said. "You just take care of yourself."

When the train finally hissed to a halt in the train yard, Eva thanked Mrs. Flanagan one last time. She walked outside into the cold and snow and climbed the steep passenger-car steps. Coal smoke stung her eyes—the potbellied stove was going full blast to heat the car. She took a seat next to a window and watched the fine snow whirl through the air. "Mama Kate," Eva whispered, "I guess this is what I get for lying." The train let out two long, loud whistles and rumbled into motion. "I'll try to be good at the orphanage so I don't get beat and so they don't take my meals away from me." She remembered Ida's stories about beatings for the smallest disobedience and being sent to bed without supper. "At least I won't have to dance anymore. And I'll have Mr. Stonewall to visit sometimes. He knows who I am, and what I've done, and what Sadie is, and he's still my friend. That's worth a lot."

The train wound down the mountains into Clear Creek Canyon and back through the foothills. As it went, the fine snow turned to wet, heavy snow and then to gray, dreary rain.

"Denver! Next stop, city of Denver!"

Eva startled awake. For a brief moment she was brought back to that first time arriving in Denver, with all of the uncertainty, fear, and hope she'd had that day.

The train ground to a halt, and the other passengers crowded the aisle. Eva sat, unmoving. On the platform she saw a large woman in a voluminous black dress and heavy cloak. *That must be Mrs. Matilda Hinsley,* she thought. Eva peered through the smudges on the window to try to read the woman's face. Was there a bit of kindness there? Or true cruelty? She couldn't tell. And she couldn't bring herself to leave the train.

The passenger car emptied out. A conductor marched down the aisle. He stopped next to her and frowned. "Miss, your ticket says Denver, and here we are."

Eva blinked at him. She made herself stand up, tucked the package of food under her arm, and walked slowly toward the end of the car.

Mrs. Hinsley had, no doubt, been alerted to her maroon gingham dress and long dark braid. She would recognize Eva as soon as she stepped out of the train. Eva felt as if she was walking into a trap, about to be captured by cruel people who would beat her and half starve her while using her to do whatever jobs they considered the most unpleasant, like changing filthy diapers and caring for sick, screaming babies.

Eva stepped off the train and glanced over at the woman she had taken to be Mrs. Hinsley. When their eyes met, the large woman gave a perturbed huff, signifying that she'd been made to wait entirely too long for Eva's appearance. She began to lumber toward Eva as if she was about to grab her by the ear and drag her off.

Eva couldn't stop herself. "Forgive me, Mama Kate!" she cried, and took off running. She dodged people and luggage, looking back only once to see Mrs. Hinsley waddling, red faced, coming after her.

Eva was halfway down Delgany Street before she even gave a thought as to *where* she was going. She stopped, out of breath. There was really only one place she could go. She turned onto 21st Street and headed toward Wazee Street and the Kansas Pacific railroad station.

Eva glanced at the skull, looking rather comfortable in its wool hat, smoking its cigar. She remembered her first day in Denver and how the skull had been a frightful sight. Now, after all she'd been through, it seemed tame.

Mr. Stonewall approached, concentrating on his work. He carried a pail and was emptying the contents of the spittoons into it. "Mr. Stonewall," Eva called.

Mr. Stonewall looked up. He blinked in disbelief. "Miss Eva!" he exclaimed.

Eva ran to him and threw her arms around his neck.

"I didn't expect you back so soon for a visit," said Mr. Stonewall. He pulled away from her, set down the pail, and held her by the shoulders. "How you been getting along?" he asked, grinning.

"I got no place to go!" Eva blurted out. "Well, maybe one place, but now I'm sure to start with a beating if I go there, on account of I ran away from Mrs. Hinsley."

Mr. Stonewall shook his head, confused. "Who's this Mrs. Hinsley? I thought you done run away from Miss B and went to Mrs. Santini. I never heard of a Hinsley in there anywhere."

A white man with a gray beard and mustache came across

the platform straight toward them. He looked angry. "Stonewall, get the shovel and the mop. For crying out loud, I tell people, 'No livestock on the passenger trains,' but do they listen? No. A fella brought in not one but *two* hogs. Both of them just did their business, and we got people stepping in it like it's a pigsty at the country fair."

Mr. Stonewall gave the man a quick nod. "Miss Eva," he said in a hushed voice, "that there's Mr. Franklin Pierce, and when he's fired up, I like to move fast. I'll be back in a minute, and don't you worry. I got friends in the police department, so I'll get you in to see your mama and sister."

"Get me in to see them?" Eva echoed, not sure what he meant.

"City jail don't normally allow visitors," said Mr. Stonewall, "but like I said, I got friends." He hoisted the shovel, mop, and a bucket of soapy water and was off.

Eva groaned, flopped down on the bench, and buried her head in her hands. "Mama Kate, I've done it *all wrong*—every last thing. I haven't made you glad, and now Sadie and Pearl are in jail for *my* debt!" She balled up one fist and jammed it down on the bench. A man in a suit walked by and gave her a suspicious sideways look. Eva decided she'd better continue her conversation with Mama Kate in silence. *When Mr. Stonewall says this is a man's town, he's not kidding. Why couldn't I just have been born a boy!? Then I could go work in the mines the way Carlos does. He sends money to his family every week. Or I could be a cowhand. They make enough money to get drunk and gamble it away every time they come into town. I could pay back those debts easy. I don't know what I'm going to do, Mama Kate, but I reckon if I'm strong enough to fight off a mountain lion, I should be able to pay back a few debts. And I'm fed up with not making you glad, so I'm fixing to do that from here on in, too.*

By the time Mr. Stonewall returned with his mop, shovel, and bucket—which now smelled like a barnyard—Eva knew one thing she needed to do.

"Mr. Stonewall," she said. "Can you take me to see Sadie and Pearl as soon as you get off work?"

The city jail, on 13th Street, still reeked of stale blood from its days as the Butterick Meat Market. Mr. Stonewall spoke quietly with the jail guard, pointed to Eva, then motioned toward the doorway that led to the holding cells. The jailer nodded, jangled his ring of keys, and disappeared through the doorway.

Eva heard Pearl first. "I don't want to talk to her, don't want to see her. She's been off having a grand time while we rot in here!"

Then Sadie's voice, a low, calming murmur.

Finally Sadie emerged alone, led by the jailer. She wore one of her fancy white gowns, but it was dirty and stained. She looked thinner, and her hands were cuffed in front of her. Eva wanted to shrink away with shame.

"Oh, Sadie," Eva cried, "I should have stayed, should never have left until I'd paid my whole debt. I'm so sorry I got you put in jail!"

Sadie frowned. "Who said you got me put in jail?" she demanded.

Eva was caught up short. "Um—nobody said. I just knew."

Sadie smiled slightly and came to Eva. She lifted both her hands, since they were cuffed together, and touched Eva's bangs. "You gave yourself a new hairstyle. I like it." Then she peered more closely and brushed Eva's hair back. She stared at the angry red scars. "When you disappeared, I thought you'd run off and got yourself killed," she said. "Looks like you almost did."

Eva cast her eyes down. "Almost," she said.

"Listen, Eva, I don't know what put it in your mind that you got us in here, but it ain't so. It's nothing to do with you and everything to do with Miss B and—" Sadie stopped and glanced at the jailer, who was listening in as if he was part of the conversation. Eva gave Mr. Stonewall a pleading look, and he got the hint.

"So, Joe, tell me about that showdown with Billy the Kid out in New Mexico last July." Mr. Stonewall put his arm around the jailer's shoulders and led him to the other side of the room. "I heard there was bullets flying everywhere and Billy *still* got away!"

Sadie began again, speaking slightly above a whisper. "There was a raid—just a normal one. They rounded up a bunch of us girls from Holladay Street and hauled us in here."

"But Pearl told me Miss B always bails out all of her girls after just one night. Mr. Stonewall said you've been in for more than a week!"

Sadie nodded. "She's trying to break Pearl—trying to break me, too, I reckon. She won't post bail until Pearl says she'll work upstairs."

Eva was flooded with relief. Them being in jail wasn't her fault after all *and* Pearl had escaped the upstairs work without running away, just like she said she would. "I'm glad Pearl didn't have to—" Eva began.

"Oh, it wasn't for Miss B not trying," said Sadie. Her eyes danced with mischief. "Miss B lost one customer. He ran out of the house screaming, afraid for his life. Pearl put the carving knife back in the kitchen before Miss B caught her with it."

Sadie grinned, and Eva burst out laughing.

"Time's almost up," the jailer said loudly.

Eva heard Mr. Stonewall stalling for time, asking more questions about Billy the Kid.

chapter twenty-one

"What will it take to get you out of here?" Eva whispered urgently.

Sadie shrugged. "Bail money, plain and simple."

The jailer marched over, took Sadie's arm, and began to lead her away.

"Tell Pearl . . . ," Eva began. "Tell her 'hey' for me."

Sadie nodded. "I will."

As if she wants to hear "hey" from me, Eva thought. But one of them had to start being friendly, and it might as well be her.

"**I**t's a poor man's supper," said Mr. Stonewall by way of apology. He uncovered the pot of beans that had kept warm on the stove all day.

"It smells wonderful," said Eva. She stirred the batter for corn bread and poured it into a pan. Mr. Stonewall had a whole stack of baking pans for her to choose from, and she remembered how he'd said his Alice did love to bake. "We'll have my peaches for dessert," she said.

Mr. Stonewall opened the oven to put the corn bread in, and a burst of heat warmed the room. "Now, Miss Eva, are you going to tell me why you look like you almost been scalped?"

"Mrs. Flanagan said my hair would cover the scars," Eva complained.

Mr. Stonewall nodded. "It will, once you heal a mite more."

As they sat waiting for the corn bread to bake, Eva told him all of it: not being able to find Mrs. Santini, being attacked by the mountain lion, recuperating at the Flanagans', and finally being sent back to Denver to the Orphans' Home.

Mr. Stonewall took it all in, commenting only with a raised eyebrow here, a grunt of surprise there. When she was done, Eva looked around the room. What in the world had she been thinking, coming to Mr. Stonewall as a way to escape the Or-phans' Home? He had only this small room, only the one bed. She remembered what he'd said when she first arrived, that if his Alice were still alive, they would take her in, but as it was, he couldn't. He'd said that he only earned enough to keep him alive and hungry. With a sinking feeling in her chest, she spoke softly. "I guess I'll get on over to the Orphans' Home this evening before too late."

Mr. Stonewall looked at her hard. "Does that kind of work suit you—taking care of babies and all?"

Eva shook her head. "I never have taken to other folks' ba-bies. Though I'm sure I'll take to my own someday. And at the home I won't get paid, so I still won't be able to pay back any-thing I owe."

Mr. Stonewall checked the corn bread and pronounced it done. They sat together at the small table and bowed their heads, and Mr. Stonewall said grace. "Lord, thank you for bring-ing Miss Eva here to see me, and please bless this food. Amen."

As he ladled beans into two bowls, Mr. Stonewall said, "Miss Eva, I want to tell you about something." He took a mouthful of beans, chewed thoughtfully, and then began. "Long time ago, back before the war started, I was in a place like you are now. I'd run away from my master, thought he owned me, just like you done run away from your mistress, thought she owned you.

"I run off in the night, like you did. Didn't know where I was headed except for one thing—follow the North Star. Everyone said that star led to freedom, and my daddy showed me how to find it. That's all I knew." He pushed back in his chair, his face half in shadow, half in the light of the kerosene lamp. "I went north from Mississippi, and round about the time I got to Missouri, I liked what I was hearing about the Kansas Territory. I heard that out here, there was lots of open spaces, not too many laws, black folks and white folks living side by side, and plenty of work to be had. I figured a place like that suited me just fine, so I picked a different star and headed west. That's how I ended up in Denver, Kansas Territory—back before Colorado was a state."

He took a sip of water. "Miss Eva, you done figured out that old dance hall doesn't suit you one bit. But you got two strong hands and two good legs and a good mind. You take a look around you, there'll be somebody needs something they'll be willing to pay you for." He raised one eyebrow. "Something *respectable*. You just figure out what suits you first. Then you'll know."

Eva looked down at her hands. "Working on the homestead suited me—with the animals and the house and the garden. I loved it because me and Mama Kate and Daddy Walter, we were building something, making a home out of nothing but prairie. And we made it better each year." She hesitated a moment, remembering. "It smelled like hay and soap and sunshine in the clothes we washed." She shook her head. "But there's nobody who needs that kind of work done in this town. And there's no one to build anything *with*."

"Unless you want to count one mama, Sadie, and one sister, Pearl, who are in need of honest work," said Mr. Stonewall.

"I'd have to get them out of jail first. I've got no money for that!"

"Some things seem impossible when they're not," he said. "Take, for instance, me getting free and coming all the way out here. That sure seemed impossible before I started. You think on it a bit."

Eva couldn't see how thinking on it would make anything seem more possible, but she didn't argue. The food and warmth of the room had made her eyelids droop. She yawned. "I better get to the Orphans' Home now," she said.

"Miss Eva, you look too tired to walk anyplace just now. You lie down in that bed. I'm going to sit up awhile. I'll wake you when it's time for me to get some sleep, and I'll walk you to the home."

Eva crawled in under the covers and thought a bed never felt so soft.

It was dawn when Eva awoke. Her sleepy brain struggled to make sense of her surroundings. Where was she? Still at Mr. Stonewall's? She sat up. There, across the room, Mr. Stonewall was slumped in a chair, his head limp, his mouth hanging open grotesquely. Horror shot through her. She leaped out of bed. "No!" she cried. She grasped his bony shoulders, shook him hard. "Mr. Stonewall! You can't be—"

Mr. Stonewall startled, snorted, opened his eyes. "What?" he said groggily. "What can't I be?"

Eva wilted with relief. "Dead."

Mr. Stonewall laughed. "Not last I looked," he said. Then he added, "Miss Eva, there's some good years left in this old body, so you don't got to worry. Did you sleep well?"

"Yes, thank you," she said. "But I didn't think you were giving up your bed for the whole night."

He winked. "I know you didn't."

"I guess I'll head over to the Orphans' Home today," Eva said. She fidgeted nervously. "Will you come visit me there, Mr. Stonewall? If they won't let me leave to visit you, will you come there?"

Mr. Stonewall patted her hand. "It's not a jail, Miss Eva, it's a safe place to stay. And I promise we'll get some visiting time one way or another." He lifted the cloth off the leftover corn bread and cut two pieces for their breakfast. "Except you haven't told me yet if you got any thoughts on work that does suit you—unless you decided overnight that you just love taking care of sick, screaming babies." A smile tried to creep onto the corner of his mouth, but he stopped it.

Just then, Eva heard the familiar shout of the water delivery-man. Mr. Stonewall grabbed coins from his coin box and two empty crockery jugs and went outside to meet the delivery truck. When he returned, Eva said, "If I'd known you had to buy water, I could have filled your jugs at Miss B's when I lived there. We had piped water right in the kitchen."

Mr. Stonewall shook his head. "Don't reckon Miss B would have liked that much—that piped water ain't free either."

Eva frowned. "Mr. Stonewall, I did think on what you said about figuring out what suits me and how some things seem im-possible but really they're not . . . but it's so darned hard to live in this town! You have to pay for *everything*—even water, and every stitch of food because you've got no place for chickens or a garden, and every bit of fuel because there's no cow pies to gather, and—"

Mr. Stonewall held up one hand. "Miss Eva, you been com-plaining to high heaven about all the things that are broke in your life. Let me ask you this: If you could fix one thing, what would it be?"

Eva didn't even have to think twice. "I'd get Sadie and Pearl out of jail."

He nodded. "Good. Why don't you work on that today?"

"You mean do a jailbreak!?" Eva nearly shouted it.

Mr. Stonewall laughed. "I was thinking more along the lines of finding bail money, but if you're in the mood to break them out, that would be cheaper." He stood and brushed crumbs from his shirt. "It's time for me to get on to work."

"Mr. Stonewall, where am I supposed to find bail money?" Eva asked, bewildered by his reasoning.

"I'm sure Miss B has got plenty, for one."

Eva's eyes bugged out. "*And* she's got designs on Pearl if she does bail them out."

"That Miss B, she's running a business, and it sounds to me like Miss Pearl is *bad* for the upstairs business." Mr. Stonewall put on his jacket and adjusted his hat on his head. "You never know until you ask," he said, and was out the door.

Eva stared after him, her jaw hanging slightly open. She shook her head. "Mama Kate, that man is crazy. He thinks I should just waltz on into Miss B's house and ask her for bail money for Sadie and Pearl *and* tell her that Pearl still won't be working upstairs. She'll laugh in my face. Plus he thinks I ought to figure out what suits me the way he did when he found the right star to follow. I sure don't know what good that'll do me."

Eva washed the corn bread pan and breakfast dishes, being

careful not to use too much of Mr. Stonewall's water. Then she took out the coins she still had left from the money he'd given her and put them into his coin box. She wouldn't be needing them at the orphanage.

She dried the dishes slowly—she was in no hurry to arrive at the Orphans' Home and receive the beating she'd get for running away from Mrs. Hinsley. As she put the dishes away, she hit upon an idea. What if she did ask Miss B for the bail money and told her to add it to her debt? What if she promised that once she was a little older and could leave the orphanage on her own, she would find a job? She'd heard that the mills in the East were hiring young girls—maybe she'd have to leave Colorado, but she would do whatever was necessary. She would send money back until her debt was paid in full, including the bail money. What if Miss B turned out to be in a good mood and agreed? Or, worse, what if Eva didn't even try and just went to the orphanage and never knew if she could have gotten Sadie and Pearl out of jail? The more she thought about it, the more it seemed she *had* to go talk to Miss B.

Eva smoothed the front of her dress and redid her braid. She looked at her reflection in the small, dim mirror hanging next to the stove. "Mama Kate, I know it sounds like a harebrained idea to go begging to Miss B but Mr. Stonewall says that I shouldn't think anything is impossible and that I won't know until I ask. Anyhow, I don't think I have anything to lose by it." Then suddenly a thought struck her with such a chill, it made it hard to breathe. What if Miss B demanded that she come back to work in the dance hall? What if Miss B snatched her by the arm and said now she would force her to work upstairs? Eva's mouth went dry. She watched her reflection in the mirror as she untied the kerchief from around her neck. Gingerly she touched the ugly scabs still left there from the mountain lion's raking claws. Then she lifted her bangs to reveal jagged, lumpy red scars. She tied her hair back with the kerchief so that the scars were fully visible. "There," she said, satisfied. "Miss B won't want me for dancing or anything else, not looking like this."

If people stared at her as she walked up Blake Street, Eva didn't notice. She walked with determination, like someone who knew in her bones that she was doing the right thing. She cut across to Holladay Street and marched up to 518. Her hand shook a bit as she raised it to knock, but she steadied herself and rapped on the door. She was glad that Lucille and the other girls would still be asleep. She didn't want to worry them with her nasty-looking scars.

Martha opened the door, took one look at Eva, and said, "I'll go get Miss B."

Eva's stomach churned as she stood in the foyer, waiting. The odor of stale cigar smoke hung in the air. She remembered that same smell clinging to her hair and clothes as she trudged up the steps after a night in the dance hall. She shook her head to dislodge the dark memories. It was all she could do to stop herself from fleeing out the door and never coming back. *There's a chance she'll agree to bail them out,* she told herself. *It's possible—I can't miss out on that.*

Miss B came sweeping into the foyer in a high-necked dress made of midnight blue silk. She narrowed her eyes at Eva.

"Martha said you've dragged yourself back here looking all chewed up. I'd have to agree."

Eva jutted out her chin. "I haven't come *back*. I'm only here to ask for you to add something to my debt. I promise that no matter what it takes, I will pay you."

Miss B scoffed. "So, you came to ask for money? From *me*? After all I did for you, and then you answered my kindness by running away? You're even more stupid than I thought." She huffed and turned to go.

"Wait!" Eva took a step forward. "The money isn't for me. It's for . . . I want to ask you to bail Sadie and Pearl out of jail. I'll pay. When I can. Even if I have to go east to work in a mill. I promise I will do it, or . . . or you can put *me* in jail."

Oh, Lord, what was she saying? Volunteering to go to jail? But the words were already out of her mouth.

Miss B eyed her. "This job you're planning to get—the one in the mill back east—are you taking Sadie and Pearl with you? Do you have a sponsor to bring you into the mill and pay your train fare? Do you know what your salary will be, how much you can send to me on a weekly basis?"

Eva's mind reeled. She hadn't thought all this through! Should she say yes and hope she could make it happen? But the last time she lied, it bought her a train ticket to an orphanage, so she dared not lie now.

"No, I have no sponsor. I was just hoping . . ."

chapter twenty-four

"Ha!" Miss B scowled at her. "All a pipe dream, as I thought. Do you think money comes from dreams? It certainly does not. If you talk to that old hag mother of yours or your uppity sister, tell them their belongings—the little that is theirs, as their gowns and jewelry belong to me—are being packed up to make room for two young ladies who will be happy to work in my establishment. When they are turned out of jail after serving their sentence—is it one year? It might be two or three, I'm not sure. Anyway, at that time they may come to me for their things."

"How could you leave them in that filthy jail?!" Eva cried. Then, seeing that Miss B would not be moved by pity, she decided to talk business. "They'll have no way of paying you back from jail, you know. If you bail them out, at least they'll have a chance of finding jobs—"

Miss B crossed her arms over her chest. "The day you come to me with a report that you've found employment for a washed-up whore and an uneducated, headstrong girl"—she laughed with contempt—"that's the day you'll see me shell out bail money for those two worthless wenches. Now get out of my house."

Eva backed away, then turned and ran through the door and down the porch steps. Outside, she blinked back tears. "Mama Kate, at least I tried," she whispered. She walked slowly down the street. "But Sadie and Pearl will be in that dirty jail for *years* now. I wish I could have helped."

Faintly Eva thought she heard someone calling her name.

For a moment she had a glimmer of hope that Miss B had changed her mind. But when she looked back, the door to 518 Holladay Street remained closed.

She heard it again, closer this time. "Miss Eva!" And footsteps. Eva turned and saw someone trotting toward her. Carlos!

She wrenched off the kerchief, pulled her bangs forward, and tied the cloth sloppily around her neck. She pasted on a smile.

"Miss Eva," Carlos said, catching up to her, out of breath. "I been looking for you. I saved my quarters and came for a dance, like I said I would, but you weren't there." He was smiling shyly, obviously happy to see her.

Eva fussed with her bangs, hoping that they were covering her scars. "I don't dance there anymore," she said.

But Carlos had noticed what she was trying to hide. He tipped his head down, looked up at her forehead. "You had an accident?" he asked gently.

She nodded. "Sort of an accident. I accidentally fought with a mountain lion."

Carlos's eyes widened. "And you won. I'd hate to see what you did to that lion!"

Eva realized he was giving her a compliment. She liked the way he put it. Yes, she had won the fight—she had survived.

"You are *una leóna valiente*," he said, "a brave lioness."

Eva smiled.

"So I still have my quarters saved," said Carlos. "When can I dance with you?"

"Oh, I don't dance for work anymore," said Eva. "You don't have to pay to dance with me."

"Really?" Carlos asked. "I can dance with you for free?"

Eva remembered how lovely it had been to flow across the floor with Carlos leading her in the circles and sweep of a dance. "I would love to dance with you for free," she said.

Carlos put down the lunch pail he had been carrying. He held out his arms. "Now?" he asked.

Eva quickly glanced around them. Morning sun glinted orange off the tops of storefronts and houses. A man drove lazily by in a Queen Ice Company wagon, the horse's hooves clopping on the packed dirt. The sign that said Holladay Street seemed to shiver as a brisk wind blew against it.

Carlos didn't wait for Eva to answer. He simply took her hand in his, laid his other hand on her waist, and, humming softly, led her in a graceful waltz. When they were done, Eva had to laugh.

"I'm going for breakfast," said Carlos. "I would like to spend my quarters to buy you a meal now that I didn't have to spend them on that dance."

But Eva shook her head. She needed to deliver herself to the orphanage—stalling was only making it harder. "Thank you, but I've already eaten," she said. "And . . . I have to be someplace."

Carlos looked so disappointed she quickly added, "I'll walk with you, though."

Carlos held out his arm, and Eva slipped her arm through his. Part of her wanted to tell him she would be at the Denver Orphans' Home so that he could visit her whenever he came to town. But a stronger part of her was too ashamed to admit where she would be living.

As they walked, Carlos made conversation. "This is my new lunch pail," he said brightly, holding up the oblong metal container. "My old one got crushed in the mine—but this one is better." He stopped and lifted the top off to show her how two metal pans were stacked neatly inside the main container to form three layers. "The bottom is for tea, the middle for stew, and the top is for a meat pie and my spoon," he said proudly.

"It's very nice," Eva said. She wondered how he could talk so calmly about his old lunch pail being crushed. Surely he was nearby when it happened. It could just as easily have been his head. "Is it scary to work in the mines?" she asked.

"Not much," Carlos said, and launched into an explanation of how they emptied out the ore in carts and then set dynamite to blast through more ore. By the time he was done, Eva was no longer jealous that she couldn't work in the mines.

They neared Camelleri's restaurant. "Are you sure you won't eat with me?" Carlos asked. "That Mrs. Camelleri is a very good cook."

Eva read the sign out front: ALL MEALS PREPARED BY MRS. CAMELLERI HERSELF. She shook her head sadly, remembering a day when Mrs. Santini and Mama Kate had called *her* a good cook. That seemed like so very long ago.

A line was already forming for the eating house. "She must be some cook," Eva said. "There's always a line here, but not at Bredenburg's or at Newby's or—"

"That's because it's men cooking at those other places," said Carlos. "We eat enough of our own cooking in the mining camps!"

Eva looked at the line of men and back at the sign. She grasped Carlos's arm. "I've got to go," she said quickly. "I've got an idea."

She ran all the way back to 518 Holladay Street.

By noon Sadie and Pearl were out of jail. By five P.M. they had been to the train station and asked Mr. Stonewall for permission to use his kitchen, found an old piece of lumber just the right size for making a sign, and cut Eva's silver dollar out of her petticoat to buy lard, flour, salt, and a jar of black paint. At five-thirty Eva and Pearl stood in Mr. Stonewall's small room, their arms powdered up to the elbows with flour. From inside the oven came the smell of baking biscuits. Sadie came in from outside with black paint smudged on her hands and face. "The sign is done," she said. "I painted it just the way you wrote it out for me: BISCUITS AND HOT GRAVY, 25 CENTS. PREPARED BY WOMEN. BRING YOUR OWN LUNCH PAIL. It's propped out front now."

Eva's hands shook, but she kept them moving. "This is how Mama Kate taught me to make gravy when you don't have any meat," she said as Pearl and Sadie watched. "You burn the flour in some lard like this. . . ." The pan sizzled, someone pounded on the door, and the three of them looked at each other wide-eyed. Sadie rushed to open the door.

"Excuse me, Miss?" A man stood with his hat in one hand and his lunch pail in the other. "Are them hot biscuits and gravy ready yet?"

● ● ●

chapter twenty-five

Mama Kate, I think I'm finally making you glad.

It's not that we have so much—just the one rented room on Larimer Street. We've also got four eating tables with chairs that Mr. Stonewall built for us and twenty plates and sets of utensils we bought with the money from selling Pearl's silver hair combs. That Pearl is a sneaky one—I don't know how on earth she got ahold of those combs, since Miss B stood over her and Sadie looking like a witch the whole time they were in there getting their things. She said that bailing them out was the last bit of kindness they'd see from her and if we didn't pay on our debt every week, we'd all three be in jail. But like Mr. Stonewall says, that Miss B is a business-woman, and I could tell from the glint in her eye that she thought I'd come up with a good idea. I'm the one who delivers her the money each week on account of Sadie and Pearl both said they've seen enough of that woman for a lifetime.

Pearl can still be ornery at times, but mostly she has forgiven me for everything: for showing up at Miss B's in September, for running away in October, and for being born in the first place.

We still get to hear the gossip from Miss B's house because Lu-cille and Ida and Ruby come eat at our place every Sunday. They say my stews are about the best they've ever had, especially my chicken cacciatore. I haven't had to make burnt flour gravy since those first few days. Sadie is best at baking—said she learned it from her mama back before she left the farm. The miners and cowhands all say she makes the most scrumptious pies this side of the Arkansas River. Pearl does the marketing and brings out the platters during meal-times. She also flirts so much with the customers that sometimes I'd swear she thinks she's back at Miss B's.

At night we roll our bedrolls out on the floor next to the eating tables, and we wash up in the morning in the kitchen sink. If we didn't have to make payments to Miss B every week, we could afford to rent a sleeping room with real beds by now. But Sadie says it's still much better than the room she rented when she first came to Denver. We keep the stove burning all night, so it's toasty warm.

Carlos comes to see me whenever he's in Denver. We go for walks, and he spends his quarters on ice cream and fruit for the two of us. He says that soon he wants to take me to a public dance, and I will be happy to go with him.

I wrote Mrs. Santini another letter, telling her how I have a good place to stay and I don't need to come to Leadville after all. I finally got a letter back—she said it was hard to find someone to write in English for her—and she said she was glad because Leadville wasn't a very good place for a young girl.

I know you'd be happier if I could get myself to school, Mama Kate, but there just isn't time for that. I did find a place that's a lot like school, though. The city of Denver has a public library with loads of books and newspapers and a reading room. I figure I can teach myself just about anything at that library.

We finally had some extra money and I sent part of mine to the Flanagans for Doc Pollock, gave part to Mr. Stonewall for his grave money, and spent the rest on calico so I could make a new dress. Then I washed Mr. Stonewall's Alice's dress, ironed it, and gave it back to him. Now it's safe in his trunk again, holding his memories.

Mr. Stonewall comes to visit about every day. He helps out wherever we need him, like painting WILKINS, LEWIS & LEWIS *in our window so everyone knows this is our eating house. He and I like to find a quiet corner, just before the suppertime rush, where we can sit and talk and eat a bowl of leftover stew. When I told him that a reporter from the* Rocky Mountain News *wants to write about our eating house, he laughed out loud. He said, "This ain't Mississippi, and it ain't heaven neither. But today, this here Colorado is looking mighty fine."*

So, Mama Kate, I'm doing good with what you said—I'm being proud and strong and living like I know in my bones that nobody in their right mind better try and push me where I don't want to go. I guess now you and Daddy Walter can go on to heaven if you want. But if you could stay and keep watch over me, maybe at least until I'm all the way grown, that would be even better.

THE ROCKY MOUNTAIN NEWS
December 3, 1878

Traveler and workingman alike will find rest and refreshment at a newly established eating house on Larimer Street in Denver. Do not be fooled by the humble window, adorned with only a simple sign, stating the names of the proprietors to be found therein: WILKINS, LEWIS & LEWIS.

Is this Mr. Wilkins and, perhaps, the Lewis brothers, toiling over the flaming stove like those much-maligned "cooks" who practice their dubious talents upon the poor cowhands who are at their mercy for months on end? Or are these three men who have sharpened their skills on the open cook fires of the mining camps here to inflict gastric disaster on unsuspecting customers?

Quite the contrary. *Miss* Wilkins, *Miss* Lewis, and *Mrs.* Lewis daily apply their considerable culinary artistry in preparing a satisfying repast as only a woman can. Though the fare is neither fancy nor elegant, diners will delight in a full menu, from sumptuous stews and hearty breads to the most delicate and tempting of pies, cakes, and custards.

Come one, come all, to the Wilkins, Lewis & Lewis eating house at 494 Larimer Street in Denver, Colorado.

author's note

In November 2000, I was in Arizona on a rock-climbing trip at Cochise Stronghold. On a rainy day (when we couldn't climb), my climbing partner and I decided to drive into Tombstone, the nearest town. We stopped in to see the "Shoot-out at the O.K. Corral" exhibit, and my attention was drawn to a book about the fallen women of the Old West. As I flipped through the pages of the book, I was riveted by a photograph of a young girl, "Jackie." The caption said that she began her career as a prostitute at "age 15," but the photograph is obviously of a much younger girl, probably twelve or thirteen years old. I couldn't take my eyes off her face—so innocent and yet determined and somehow worldly. I wanted, desperately, to save her.

My mind began to race with questions: What pressures had caused Jackie to choose this profession? With the right help, could she have made a different choice? How was she like the young girls of today, who, at younger and younger ages, are feeling pressured into becoming sexually active? I knew I had to write a story about Jackie and give her a chance to choose a different path. That was how, at least in my imagination, I would be able to reach back in time and save this young girl. At the same time, I hoped to create a parable for modern young readers that might offer them the strength and insight to choose their own different path. Jackie, of course, became Eva.

The pressures of economic survival that plagued the girls and women of the Old West are akin to the social pressures and need for love and acceptance that young girls are faced with today. It is my hope that this story can act as a bridge from past to present and as a springboard for discussion.

Though all of the main characters in *Last Dance on Holladay Street* are fictitious, some of the peripheral characters are real people. Mattie Silks and Belle Birnard were real Denver madams who operated brothels on Holladay Street. Much more has been written about Mattie Silks elsewhere, as she is an integral part of Denver's history. Billy the Kid really was involved in a shootout in Lincoln, New Mexico, in July of 1878, and Mary Gallagan really was arrested for having girls ages eleven and thirteen working in her brothel—upstairs.

For further reading about Denver's ladies of the evening, I would recommend *Hell's Belles: Denver's Brides of the Multitudes* by Clark Secrest. For information on the black experience in the Old West, see *Black Pioneers: Images of the Black Experience on the North American Frontier* by John W. Ravage. And to find out more about what it was like to grow up on the western frontier, read *Children of the West: Family Life on the Frontier* by Cathy Luchetti. All three of these books have many wonderful photographs, are carefully researched, and will guide you to further resources.

acknowledgments

In writing *Last Dance on Holladay Street*, I wanted to re-create life in the 1870s in three parts of Colorado: in a small town on the high plains east of Denver, in Denver, and in a mountain mining town. In each of these locales, I had the privilege of working with a historian who knew the area and the culture and was willing to answer questions and brainstorm with me for hours, take me on historic tours, and, when the writing was done, read the manuscript to help check for accuracy. My heartfelt thanks goes out to, on the high plains, Terry Blevins of the Lincoln County Historical Society in Hugo, Colorado; in Denver, Gwendolyn Crenshaw, library manager of the Blair-Caldwell African American Research Library; and in the mountain town of Georgetown, Christine Bradley, county archivist for Clear Creek County.

In addition, I would like to thank my good friends Wayne and Alice C. Gilbert, who put me up for at least part of every one of my five research trips to Colorado and also gave input on the story and manuscript, and Lee Behrens, regional director of the Colorado Historical Society, who took me on a private tour of the Lebanon Mine and helped me track down the remains of the old Plume Hill road and the tollhouse that Eva walked by.

Many thanks to the following people who patiently answered my many questions: Kenton Forrest and Charles Albi, archivists at the Colorado Railroad Museum library; Charleszine "Terry" Nelson, senior special collections manager at the Blair-Caldwell African American Research Library; Janet Bernadyn, curator at the Hamill House Museum/Historic Georgetown, Inc.; Paul and Sally Nisler, owners of the historic Rose Street Bed and Breakfast in Georgetown; Alexandra Flinn, who helped me with the songs of the period; and Dora Mae Vassios, librarian at the Hugo Public Library.

I would also like to thank the research assistants at these Denver research facilities: the Denver Public Library (Western History Department), the Colorado History Museum, the Colorado Historical Society research library, the Black American West Museum and Heritage Center, and the Tattered Cover Book Store.

I am very grateful to my niece, Gena Carbone, my husband, Jim, and my father, Dad, for repeated readings of the manuscript as it went through many editorial changes. And I owe special thanks to the editors and assistant editors who worked with me on this book: Tracy Gates and Rachel Nugent, who saw it through its birth and early stages, and Joan Slattery and Jamie Weiss, who guided the story through its growing pains and changes and on to maturity.

Elisa Carbone is the acclaimed author of several books for young readers, including *Storm Warriors,* the winner of the 2002 Jefferson Cup Award and an ALA Notable; *Stealing Freedom,* an ALA Best Book for Young Adults; *Sarah and the Naked Truth;* and *The Pack.* She normally lives in Maryland and West Virginia, but during the years she worked on *Last Dance on Holladay Street,* she spent months in Colorado researching, writing, rock climbing, and skiing.

For more information about Elisa Carbone and her work, visit her Web site at www.elisacarbone.com.